Praise for *Mrs. Gari Melchers*

"*Mrs. Gari Melchers* follows Corinne Melchers' steadfast journey for recognition in a society that expects women to stay in the background. From art school critiques to the unforgiving Paris Salon, and a life with renowned painter Gari Melchers in Holland, Corinne must reconcile her identity as an artist, a wife, and a woman fighting to be seen. She builds a creative life alongside, and sometimes despite, a husband who loves her dearly but struggles to understand her yearnings, despite being an artist himself. Joyce Miller's beautifully crafted historical novel is a nuanced, heartfelt exploration of ambition, marriage, and the quest for artistic freedom in an era in which women's voices often were not heard. Miller offers a moving portrait of resilience, quiet defiance, and creative hunger."

—Gigi Howard, host of the podcast *Drinks in the Library*

"For lovers of art and Virginian history, Joyce Miller's *Mrs. Gari Melchers* offers a glimpse into a world gone by. Grounded in period and technical detail, the opening scenes transport the reader into the early twentieth century life of Corinne Mackall, an artist who struggles to find her place amid shifting feminist expectations, the fetters of Depression-era societal norms, and turmoil of two world wars. In Corinne, Miller has unearthed a figure often relegated to the footnotes of art history . . . but who is clearly worth getting to know in her own right."

—Joanna Lee, Poet Laureate of Richmond, Virginia, and author of *Dissections*

Mrs. Gari Melchers

Mrs. Gari Melchers

Joyce A. Miller

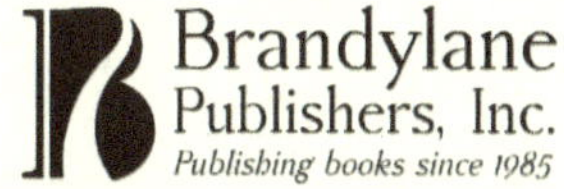
Brandylane Publishers, Inc.
Publishing books since 1985

ISBN (Paperback): 978-1-966369-40-0
ISBN (eBook): 978-1-966369-41-7
Library of Congress Control Number: 2025916247

Designed by Sami Langston
Project managed by Kaitlyn Garrett

Published by
Brandylane Publishers, Inc.
5 S. 1st Street
Richmond, Virginia 23219

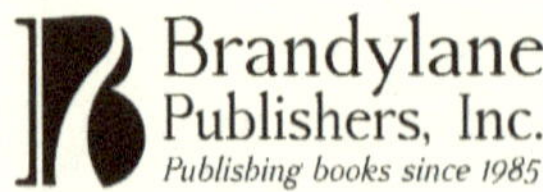

brandylanepublishers.com

Dedicated to all women who have dreamed
despite society's limitations

Contents

Author's Note

Mrs. Gari Melchers is a work of fiction. In this story, details in the lives of Corinne Melchers, Gari Melchers, and other historical figures are a product of creative license. However, at its core, this novel is based on the real life of Corinne Melchers.

While I have endeavored to maintain historical accuracy, I have occasionally altered the chronology of certain events to fit the narrative.

At times, I have quoted authentic newspaper articles. Other names, characters, places and events are products of my imagination and any resemblance to actual persons, living or dead, events, or locales is coincidental.

Acknowledgments

I am forever indebted to the following people for helping bring this story to life.

Thank you to Marilyn Paolino for reading the very early pages and pushing the book in the right direction.

Thank you to my beta readers, Kelly Patel, Emily Sattie, and Erin Breeden; and to my first editor, Zachary Steele, for your ideas on bringing Corinne's story to life.

Thank you to the Brandylane team for supporting this book.

Thank you to my author friends, Ami Hicken King and Nancy Houser Bluhm, who believed and listened and told me, "Of course you can do this!"

Thank you to the docents at Belmont who guided me on tour after tour and shared their enthusiasm for Corinne. I learned a little something on each visit.

Thank you to my husband Alan Gavalya who supported me through all the ups and downs. I love you.

And finally, thank you to my readers for spending your valuable time reading my words. I hope you enjoy Corinne's story as much as I do.

Chapter 1

1900: The Student

Corinne Mackall centered the vase of fragrant daffodils and the Delft Blue, floral teapot and sugar bowl on the dining room table. A triangle of sunlight streaming in from the nearby window illuminated one corner of the still life and made the colors dance across the mahogany wood. Satisfied, she pulled out her seat and sat down.

"Oh, for heaven's sake, Corinne, just sit down and eat your breakfast," her mother said. Corinne placed her sketchbook next to her plate and began sketching the still life in front of her.

"I just need to make a brief thumbnail sketch before I eat," Corinne said. She laid her colored pencils next to her plate as if they were silverware.

This is an interesting study, Corinne thought. She reflected on the addition of the daffodils' shades of yellow and green that the daffodils added to the scene of the blue vase and the blue and white teapot and sugar bowl. *And the height of the vase makes a nice triangular shape for the composition.*

"Just once I'd like to have a meal where we talk and eat. No sketching," her mother said.

Corinne and her mother, Louise, sat across from each other in the spacious dining room. From Corinne's end of the table, she could see from the corner of her eye the white lace curtains fluttering slightly. The maid stood quietly next to the mahogany sideboard. The delicate moss green wallpaper framed her white apron and cap. As soon as Corinne dropped her pencil, the maid served her a plate of eggs and toast and a small bowl of citrus fruit. Corinne poured herself a cup of tea from the pot at the center of the table.

Corinne blew on the tea before she took a sip.

"You're going to your studio today then, not to school?" Louise questioned.

"I have a few paintings at the studio I have to finish to take to school later this week. And it's such a beautiful day today that I think I will walk there."

"Oh, please take the carriage. What will people think?"

"You know very well that I don't care what other people think." Corinne smiled and stood up from the table. She walked over, bent down, and kissed the top of her mother's head.

She gathered her sketchbook, pinned a hat to her light brown hair, draped a jacket over her white shirtwaist and navy-blue skirt, and headed out the door of 800 Cathedral Street. She walked several blocks down Cathedral past the Baltimore Basilica and turned left to get to Charles Street. Despite staying on the sidewalk, she had to dodge the occasional horse blocking her path. Arriving at her destination, she unlocked the door and entered her studio at 347 Charles Street.

Although Corinne liked to paint landscapes as she prepared for her final class at the Maryland Institute Day School of Design, still life subjects, in varying stages of completion, surrounded her in the studio. Some canvases were leaning against walls, some were hanging on the walls, and two others were on easels. She would submit these for her final grade before graduation.

She wasted no time. She grabbed a smock, tied it over her skirt, rolled up her sleeves, and grabbed a paintbrush. When she noticed she had grabbed a brand-new paintbrush, she returned it to its place and retrieved a used one. Although not overly superstitious, she believed that starting a new painting with a new brush would bring bad luck. For each painting, she had a specific ritual. She closed her eyes and took some deep breaths as she stood in front of her easel. She unclenched her jaw and let her tongue fall from the roof of her mouth. Then she began.

Corinne hoped to turn the still life she had sketched that morning into yet another painting. She loved daffodils and was drawn to work in the Impressionist manner. The flower really does shout out that spring is on the way. She hoped that feeling would come across as she dabbed on yellow oxide, green gold, and lemon yellow to capture the color of the petals. She backed away from the painting, put one hand on her hip, and held the end of the paintbrush close to her lips. She studied her composition. *I must let go of being viciously critical of what I create and see things that I don't like as building blocks to knowing more about what I do like,* Corinne recited a familiar mantra as she worked. *I love to see the paint, feel the brush in my hands, and hear the sound of the bristles on the canvas. It sounds so simple, but it's so hard.*

Later, Corinne turned her attention to a portrait of her mother. She had begun this painting with a sepia underpainting to depict the shadows and the highlights correctly. She needed to add some color to it. Skin comprised shades of blue, green, yellow, pink, and brown. She squeezed raw sienna, Payne's gray, and titian buff onto the palette she had been using for the flowers. Cooler colors were employed in the shadows, whereas warmer tones were applied to the lips, forehead, and neck. She loved trying to capture the lights and darks, it was so tricky. She decided this portrait would be a gift for her mother, not an entry for the Salon. She hoped her mother would like it.

She was determined to succeed in the Paris art world, and that meant showing work at the Salon held in the Palace of the Louvre. After graduation, she planned to take a selection of her paintings to Paris. She understood the process. The jury would look at hundreds of paintings each day, raising their canes or umbrellas to denote acceptance. An attendant would write "A" for *admis* or "R" for *refuse* on the back. The jury ranked the accepted works, and the highest ranked work was displayed at eye level with Number two just above. And number three just above that. Higher numbers were "skyed," meaning the painting was hung far above eye level where it would be hard to see. Exhibiting at the Salon was an honor and would mean Corinne was accepted by the art world.

Corinne had recently read in the *Baltimore Sun* that Washington, DC was creating a "National Salon" to rival Paris, but the first one had been less than noteworthy. The report noted that out of five to six hundred frames, not one painting in five had surpassed mediocrity. Next to portraits from some of the finest DC painters were student drawings of seashells and landscapes. There was not a single impressionist painting. The miniatures were of the same grade as those shown at charity bazaars. After reading about it in the newspaper, Corinne was more convinced than ever that she had to go to Paris, even though Washington DC was a much easier destination for travel. Corinne wrapped her completed paintings in brown paper and headed to the school.

*

Louisa Stewart, the painting instructor, stood at the head of the class. Corinne placed the paintings on the ledge around the room with the works of the other students. She took her place at her desk and waited for the critique to begin.

Maybe I won't be famous. But that's not why I started painting. I want the world to see my paintings and feel the things that I feel, Corinne reflected.

Miss Stewart, tall and slim, walked slowly past the paintings. Her long navy skirt swished with each stride. She stopped in front of each one and her eyes scanned from left to right and top to bottom. When she reached Corinne's section, she stopped, taking a second (and even third) look at her canvas.

"Corinne, this painting is fantastic. I like how you have paid close attention to the subtleties of color within the shadows and the highlights. I feel like I could walk up to this painting and smell the daffodils," Miss Stewart said.

"Oh, perhaps I was just fortunate that day in my studio and just happened to grab the right combination of colors," Corinne blushed.

"I don't understand why you belittle yourself with that comment. What are you afraid of?" Miss Stewart asked her.

"My art reflects me. I try not to judge my efforts. But I'm afraid that if my art is not as good as the other students' artwork, then I'm not good enough." Corinne swallowed hard. Just setting up her paintings had caused her palms to sweat.

"Don't you want to exhibit paintings at the Salon?"

"Yes, but only if they're good enough. I would have to ask my mother to accompany me to Paris to take the paintings for jury. I couldn't travel there by myself. So much could go wrong. And how could I face my mother and my brothers if I were rejected?"

"Remember, with art you are always on a journey. You will never find out if they're good enough unless you submit them. That is the validation. You have the capacity for taking infinite pains and the patience required to produce beautiful art. And I can assure you that these paintings you've shown today are indeed 'good enough,'" Miss Stewart said. "They compare to paintings I've seen by Mary Cassatt and Berthe Morisot. You deserve to treat yourself with the same respect."

Shocked and honored by the compliment, Corinne's mouth fell open.

"I would like to ask some others in the class to make their remarks on your paintings," Miss Stewart said. She looked over at the group of seated women and picked one from the front row.

"Esther? Any comments?"

Esther rose from her chair and walked over to look at the paintings more closely. Esther was an enormous woman who dwarfed Corinne. She was also soft-spoken and one of the nicest students in the class.

"I see Corinne's still life florals as alive and a subject of serious art. Like Miss Stewart said, these paintings could rival Mary Cassatt's *Lilacs in a Window.* Flowers are difficult to paint well because their structure is so complicated, but you've done that here by stacking petal upon petal with thick paint but a light touch," Esther said in an angelic voice. Every time Corinne heard her speak; she found it hard to reconcile the voice with the size of the woman.

"Blooms from our own garden inspired me here. I attempted to capture the range of tones in their petals as they reflect and absorb light. It's like painting a sunrise or a sunset in each blossom," Corinne said.

"I know we're not supposed to say whether or not we like them. We're just supposed to comment on the artistic qualities of the paintings, but I like them," Esther said as she smiled in Corinne's direction.

"Thank you," Corinne responded.

Mabel, one of the other women in the class stood up. Mabel's smock was stained with many different colors of paint. Corinne looked hopefully in her direction.

"Personally, I don't want to comment on your art because it's not to my taste," Mabel said. Mabel painted in a more primitive style than Corinne.

"Art is subjective," Miss Stewart said.

"I really like the overall feel of the pieces. But there are some spots that need more work. Given the sunny mood of the painting, I'd expect to see more confident brushwork," Mabel said.

Corinne looked down at her feet as Mabel spoke.

"Please understand that I wish you the best and hope for your success," Mabel said.

Despite the relatively positive comments from her classmates, Corinne still felt that she may not be good enough for the Salon. She turned her attention back to her instructor.

"It's time, Corinne. You must take these paintings to Paris," Miss Stewart said. Corinne knew that her teacher was tough but fair and would not suggest this if she didn't think Corinne was ready. Corinne had to trust her talent and hard work. No one else besides her had to live with the consequences of her choices.

Chapter 2

1902: The Ship

"Mother, we have to hurry!" Corinne impatiently pulled on her second glove. They stood on the dock near the gangplank. The staff had already loaded their luggage and Corinne's trunk of paintings.

"I'm ready, Corinne," Louise said. The two women walked arm in arm up the gangplank. A steward from the German steamship S. S. Alier met them on deck.

"Welcome aboard, ladies," he said.

"Thank you, young man," Louise addressed him. They walked to a point along the railing to wave goodbye to the people waiting on the dock. It was an April day with a cloudless, brilliant blue sky.

"I don't really know how I let you talk me into this," Louise said.

"We've gone over it, Mother. I must take the paintings to Paris myself to be juried. I couldn't trust to send them with someone else. And I was overjoyed to find some other artists' names on the passenger list. Gari Melchers, for one. I will keep my eye open for him," Corinne said.

"Gari Melchers is at least twenty years older than you. Why would you care if he is on this ship?" Louise asked.

"I love his work. I would love to hear some of his ideas on painting if we get the chance to talk while on board," Corinne said.

"We'll be on the ship for over a week. It upsets me we're having to use some of your father's inheritance to take this trip. There will be less money for your wedding dowry," Louise said.

Corinne fell silent at that. Her father had died in a horrible carriage accident when she was ten years old. Her grandfather owned a sugar company where her father had worked as a clerk. He was driving from his home when the horses got frightened by the loud machinery noise at the mill. The spokes of the carriage wheels caught his legs and dragged him for some distance. Corinne's older brother Leonard had been on the driving seat beside him but was unhurt. Her brother told her that their father had been unconscious until he died, and she took some solace in that. Leonard couldn't bring himself to ride in a carriage afterwards and experienced nightmares. Her father had been in the Confederate calvary and had lived through the Civil War. It seemed impossible to her that he then died in such a fashion. Her mother never remarried.

"Mother, Corinne, come and see our suite of rooms," Corinne's younger brother, Lawton, called to them from next to the cabin door. With his right arm extended, he gestured comically for the two women to enter the hatch. At fourteen, Lawton was now taller than Corinne's petite, four-foot ten-inch frame. He had been so excited about his first trip to Europe that he had dashed onto the ship ahead of them.

The suite had a large living area with a couch and two armchairs. Adjacent from this room were two bedrooms decorated with silk wallpaper.

"It's just like the Belvedere Hotel in Baltimore," Corinne said as she slowly turned around inside the room.

Soon the ship set sail. Corinne and Lawton strolled along the wooden deck, occasionally leaning over the side to look at the water and to see if they could spot any dolphins racing along the side of the ship. Their mother took a nap in the cabin.

It wasn't long before they met a group of men walking towards them. All were dressed in wool trousers and jackets with round-collared white shirts. Corinne and Lawton leaned against the railing to give them room to pass. Corinne caught the eye of one of the men, and he smiled as he tipped his bowler hat to her. He was broad and burly, but also very calm and grave. She turned her attention back to Lawton.

"I wonder who those men are. Do you think one of them may be Mr. Gari Melchers?" she asked. She had seen descriptions of Gari Melchers' paintings in the art magazines at the school, but she didn't know what he looked like.

"Maybe we'll find out at dinner," Lawton replied.

A few hours later, Louise, Corinne, and Lawton entered the dining room. Louise and Corinne were dressed in floor length ball gowns. Corinne's sky-blue gown with puffed sleeves and heart-shaped bodice matched her eyes. She wore elbow-length white gloves, and she piled her auburn hair into a bun on top of her head.

A band was playing in the far corner of the dining room. When they boarded, the Mackalls had been given a billet with the dinner seats numbered. They made their way to their table. Corinne was surprised to see two men seated at their table; one of them was the man who had tipped his hat to her earlier. He was clearly much older than she was. His hair, mustache, and goatee were speckled with silver. His eyes were gray, but they had a sparkle to them that denied his years.

He stood up and held out the chair for her while his companion did the same for Louise.

"Good evening," he said. "As it looks like we'll be dinner companions for the duration of the trip, allow me to introduce myself. Gari Melchers, born in Detroit, Michigan, but currently living in North Holland. And this is George Hitchcock from Providence, Rhode Island, also living in North Holland."

"Pleased to meet you," Corinne said. "I'm Corinne Mackall. This is my mother, Louise, and my younger brother, Lawton, of Baltimore, Maryland." Corinne couldn't help but notice the paint stains on Gari's hands as he pulled out her chair.

"Enchanted to make your acquaintance, Mrs. Mackall, Master Mackall, and Miss Mackall," Gari said as they all sat down at the table.

"What kind of work do you do, Mr. Melchers?" Louise asked. Corinne cringed, knowing her mother already was fully aware of what kind of work the men did.

"Both my friend and I are artists. Painters, to be more exact. We're considered American Impressionist painters, although I'm not sure that's completely accurate. I'm just returning to Holland after teaching a four-week painting class at the School of the Art Institute of Chicago," Gari replied.

"How fascinating. Our Corinne is a painter, too," Louise said.

"Yes, I'm taking some of my paintings to see if they'll be juried into the Paris Salon," Corinne added.

"Paris is the leading city in the world for artists. I tried attending the École des Beaux-Arts there for a while," Gari said.

"He was on a bash at too many social events for him to stick with it," his friend George laughed and winked. "The French Impressionists had nothing on him."

Corinne smiled at that remark.

"Have you been to Paris before?" Gari asked.

"Mother and I have been there a few times. It's Lawton's first trip," Corinne said.

"Paris is one of my favorite cities, but after I traveled all over Europe and survived cholera in Italy, George here talked me into helping him start an art school in North Holland. The cholera made me see that life is fragile and I wanted my life to have some impact. So, I went to teach at the Egmondse School. Have you heard of it?" Gari asked. He continually made eye contact with Corinne as if she was the only one seated at the table.

"No, I'm afraid I haven't heard about your school. But how did you manage to survive cholera? It's a miracle you pulled through," Corinne said.

"Well, I learned it's better to drink wine in Italy than to drink water," Gari joked.

"It's beautiful in Holland. Symphonies of color and right on the water's edge," George interrupted.

"What do you paint? Landscapes? Still life?" Gari asked Corinne.

"Mostly I paint still life in the Impressionist style, although I like traditional realism, too. I've painted many landscapes in both styles."

"I'd like to see them."

"You can see them when they're displayed at the Salon," Corinne said in a rush of confidence. Perhaps it was Gari's undivided attention that gave her such self-assurance.

George let out a huge laugh. "Have you any idea how many paintings they deny at the Salon every year? Only a small percentage of paintings get accepted at the Salon."

Gari cut a sharp look at his friend.

Corinne took in a deep breath and slowly exhaled. She called upon the trust that her teacher and classmates had instilled in her. "That may be the case, Mr. Hitchcock. But mine will be among the ones accepted."

Gari gazed at her intently as dessert was served. He could see she wanted to establish a successful life built on her art. He knew it would be difficult for a woman.

"I'm quite full of the dinner. I believe I'll pass on the dessert and retire to our cabin. Mother, I'll see you later. Lawton, will you accompany me back? If you'll excuse me, gentlemen," Corinne said.

George and Gari stood at the table as Corinne gathered her purse and fan and left for her room. As they sat back down, they looked at one another with the realization that they had offended the young woman. Gari hoped the beautiful young painter would give him another chance to make a better impression.

The next evening at dinner, George and Gari were the first to arrive in the dining room. The ship's staff were still setting wine and water glasses on the tables. Gari continually craned his neck to watch the doorway.

"She'll be here for dinner. She and her family have to eat," George said to Gari.

Soon, the Mackall family approached the table and sat down.

"Gentlemen," Louise said.

"Miss Mackall, I believe we got off on the wrong foot yesterday. Please accept my apology," Gari said as soon as they had been seated.

"I want to be an artist, and I've denied myself many comforts to make that happen," Corinne said. "I don't want to be taken lightly."

"No, no, of course not," Gari replied.

"I'd like to hear more about your school in Holland," Corinne said, softening.

"George started it. His studio was there and at first it was a summer art school. There are beautiful Dutch gardens there, full of tulips. The landscapes, with the beaches, houses, and windmills, cry out, practically asking to be painted, George had a painting of his tulip garden accepted into the Salon," Gari said.

"That's much about George and not much about you," Corinne said.

"My father was an artist, a sculptor. I guess he instilled in me the love of art. I love painting the Dutch people, especially the women with their children. They work so hard while wearing such delightful, colorful clothes. I can't get enough of them," Gari said.

Gari then turned to Louise. "I'd love for your family to visit us in Holland, Mrs. Mackall. When you're finished with your business in Paris."

"When we finish in Paris, we are going to Austria to visit my father, Alexander Lawton. He is the Ambassador to the Austrian Court," Louise said.

"Well, when you're finished in Austria, then?" Gari was grasping at straws.

"Perhaps it can be arranged," Louise said.

After they had finished dessert, Gari turned to Louise and asked, "May I escort your daughter back to your cabin after dinner? I thought we could take a walk around the deck first."

"If it's all right with Corinne," Louise said, when she glanced in Corinne's direction and noticed the pleading look in her eyes.

"A moonlit stroll around the deck sounds wonderful," Corinne said. She had long since forgiven him for his faux pas the evening before.

Corinne took Gari's arm as they strolled along the wooden deck. He was a big, broad-shouldered man, and Corinne felt comfortable with him. A few thin clouds lingered over a moon, that lit up the surface of the water. Dozens of stars twinkled around it. The ship was moving almost noiselessly through the waves, but Corinne could still hear a few waves lapping against its side. Corinne closed her eyes and took a deep breath of the sea air.

"Stand there by the rail, Miss Mackall. I'd love to make a sketch of you." Gari pulled a sketchbook and some pencils out of his suit coat pocket. Corinne stood next to the railing as Gari sat on one of the deck chairs, scratching away in his sketchbook.

"You may call me Corinne."

"And you can call me Gari. Come and look at what I've sketched now, Corinne."

The ship made a slightly unexpected move, and they laughed as they almost bumped heads when he leaned over to show her his sketchbook.

Corinne thought he had captured the moment. She was facing away from him, gazing at the water and sky. She was thoughtfully looking towards Europe, towards a metaphorical future. She wanted to tear the sketch from the book and keep it forever.

"It's beautiful, but I must get back to my cabin now. Mother will be worried." Corinne forced herself to say.

As they neared her cabin door, Gari asked, "We'll be arriving at port soon. May I call on you in Paris? I would love to introduce you to some of the artists I know. I could even help you take your paintings to the Salon. It is a bit of a scary experience."

"That would be lovely," Corinne replied.

"Good night," Gari said. It took all his strength not to pull her into him as she looked into his eyes.

Inside the cabin, she leaned back against the door and smiled to herself. She could hear him whistling as he walked away from her door.

Corinne woke up the next morning thinking of Gari. He was one of the most interesting men she had ever met. It didn't matter that he was older than she was. He was so smartly dressed and classically handsome. She felt that his gray eyes looked at her as if she were the only person on the entire ship. She wondered if he was thinking about her in the same manner.

*

The waters of the Mediterranean were so much bluer than the Atlantic. As much as they enjoyed the ship, the family was happy to reach land. After traveling through the Atlantic and Mediterranean for a week, Corinne and Lawton spotted the Genoa lighthouse from the ship's railing. The Mackalls disembarked and headed to the train station. They boarded the express train headed from Rome to the Gare de Lyon in Paris. The Mackalls had both a dining compartment and a sleeping compartment on the train. The first-class coach was upholstered in tan leather with lace covers. They were quite comfortable having a compartment with a small table in between the seats for writing or playing cards.

"Mother, we must have petit dejeuner at Le Train Bleu, so I can see Monsieur Olive's paintings. I've heard the restaurant is opulent with blue carpets and gilded ceilings," Corinne said. She was excited to see the restaurant's large fresco which depicted some of the cities they had traveled through during the night.

"Corinne, we're tired. Let's just get a taxi to our apartment," Louise overruled her daughter. She had not slept well on the train.

As they stepped onto the street and called for a cab, the bright, golden Eiffel Tower glistened in the distance.

"To Rue des Rosiers," Louise said to the taxi driver.

They soon arrived at their first-floor apartment in the middle of the neighborhood known as Le Marais. The apartment was spacious, with high ceilings and three floor-to-ceiling windows that faced the street. Immediately, Corinne opened the draperies to let in as much light as possible.

The taxi driver began carrying in their trunks of clothing and the wooden box containing Corinne's paintings. Corinne heard a crack as he banged the box against the door frame.

"Please, be careful with that box," she said, as she ran over to check on any damage.

"Je suis desole, Mademoiselle," the driver apologized.

A few days later, Gari knocked on Corinne's door, as they had arranged beforehand. She couldn't stop smiling when she saw him.

"I'm here to take you and your paintings to the Salon. I have a carriage waiting," Gari said.

As they drew closer to the Louvre, Gari reminded her that the Impressionists were rarely selected. Gari took her hand in his and observed that it was shaking.

As Gari and Corinne entered the room, they noticed the paintings leaning face-forward against the wall, many with "A" penciled on them. Gari pulled a few of the paintings away from the wall to look at them; *A Seated Woman* by Miss Cecilia Beaux was the first work. The next was Miss Beaux's portrait of a man standing. It seemed inferior to her neighboring work but was technically proficient. The third painting Gari peeled back from the wall was a charming portrait of a standing woman in a green dress with a black background.

"Everyone stands on the shoulders of someone who has come before," Gari said. "That they've chosen Miss Beaux bodes well for you. She's another American."

"I know of Miss Beaux. She teaches at the Pennsylvania Academy.... Oh, I'm so nervous! It's also important for me to paint works I would want to view myself. I hope then that others can relate to my paintings," Corinne said.

"My friends, John Sargent and James Whistler, are also exhibiting. I've seen John's portrait, *Two Sisters.* He has such skill at infusing softness and elegance into his paintings. But there are so many portraits at this year's Salon."

"Well then, I shall stand out with my still lifes," Corinne said.

The attendants in white coats and blue caps soon lifted three of Corinne's paintings to the walls. The judges stood around them, waving their umbrellas and walking canes. Several of the judges shook their heads. All of her work received a shameful "R" scratched onto the back for "Refuse." The attendants carried Corinne's paintings out on a stretcher as if they were corpses.

Corinne hung her head. But she had learned that two things impressed the judges: the size of the painting, and human interest as a subject. Perhaps she should have brought the portrait she had done of her mother rather than the floral paintings.

"Well, now I have to go back and face Mother," Corinne said, with tears in her eyes. "She always compares me to my brother, Leonard. He's a successful writer and I'm an unsuccessful painter."

"You're not unsuccessful. You just haven't been successful this time," Gari said. "Don't give up. Come with me to Holland and paint at my school."

"But my mother is going on to Austria to visit my grandfather. I couldn't come alone without a chaperone," Corinne said.

"You could if we were engaged." Gari dropped to one knee. "I've known since the first time I saw you on the boat that I was in love with you. I want to marry you."

Did Corinne love him? He was patient and older, wiser. Was she looking for a father or a husband? She certainly didn't want things to end between them. Gari had such a confidence about him, and that made her more self-assured. Was she naïve to think that this great painter could be her husband and *also* her teacher?

"Yes, I'll marry you," she said. Corinne's tears of frustration turned to tears of joy and excitement. It surprised her that in the short time she had known Gari she trusted him completely. She was flattered that he had taken such an interest in her. No one had ever appreciated her in such a way before. Her canvas of disappointment had been unexpectedly repainted with Gari's strokes of love and promise.

Chapter 3

1903: The Egmondse School

As reported in the "Society news, Events in the Polite World" column of the *Baltimore Sun*: Mr. Gari Melchers, reknowned portrait painter, married Corinne Lawton Mackall, daughter of Mrs. Leonard Covington Mackall, at St. Brelade's Bay, Isle of Jersey.

The bridal party arrived for the ceremony by wagonettes on a Tuesday at noon at the St. Brelade's Bay Hotel on the beach. *Marry on Monday for health, Tuesday for wealth, Wednesday the best day of all, Thursday for crosses, Friday for losses and Saturday for no luck at all* was the rhyme everyone knew and loved. However, Gari and Corinne chose to marry on a Tuesday: a year to the date they met on the ship. Corinne's Matron of Honor was Henrietta Hitchcock, George's wife. George himself stood as the Best Man.

The bride, with her hand resting lightly on the arm of her older brother Leonard, entered the main hall of the St. Brelade's Bay Hotel stylishly gowned in blue-pink lightweight muslin made over taffeta and trimmed with satin. She wore a matching broad-brimmed hat that framed her face, and she carried a shower bouquet of bridal roses. Henrietta was dressed similarly, as was the custom, to confuse evil spirits and hide the true bride, thus keeping the evil spirits from ruining the wedding day.

"April 14, 1903, a year to the day that we met on the ship," Gari whispered to his lovely bride. He took her hand in front of the minister, and they repeated their vows.

"I, Julius Garibaldi Melchers, take you, Corinne Lawton Mackall, to be my wife, to have and to hold from this day forward, for better, for worse, for richer, for poorer, in sickness and in health, to love and to cherish, till death do us part, according to God's holy law, and this is my solemn vow."

"I, Corinne Lawton Mackall, take you, Julius Garibaldi Melchers, to be my husband, to have and to hold from this day forward, for better, for worse, for richer, for poorer, in sickness and in health, to love, cherish and to obey, till death do us part, according to God's holy law, and this is my solemn vow." It wasn't lost on Corinne that she was obliged to vow to obey her husband, even if they both felt they were a team taking on the world.

After the ceremony, the new Mr. and Mrs. Melchers welcomed guests at the entrance of the salon at the St. Brelade's Hotel. The great hall was wainscoted in quartered oak with a massive fireplace. A great crystal chandelier with hundreds of glittering pendants lit the scene. The bride's table was set up in the picture gallery, a room with walls covered in famous paintings. Gari had picked this room, and this hotel, especially for Corinne. A tall, silver candelabra surrounded by chrysanthemums, ferns, and carnations was a centerpiece at their table, and a pale green ribbon with the monogram "M-M" stretched from the centerpiece to each place setting. Couples filled the dance floor to waltz. An orchestra played throughout the evening. The couple spent their first night as man and wife in the most luxurious suite of the hotel, but Corinne looked forward to a painting honeymoon at the Egmondse school.

*

After the wedding celebration, Gari travelled ahead of Corinne to prepare the home for her arrival. They wrote letters to each other every day. When his letters arrived, she could hardly wait to open them.

> Dear Corinne,
>
> Such wonderfully sweet and dear letters as you do write me. I would just like to squeeze and kiss and hug you for every single word you say.
>
> Yours forever,
>
> Gari

The month of May was the sunniest time of the year and a lovely time to arrive at the Egmondse School. The tulip and flower gardens exploded in blue, red, pink, and violet. From her perch atop the dunes, she gazed down at the small fishing village. The sea air washed over her, carrying a sharp, clean scent. Wives and children of the fishermen knitted fishing nets with large wooden needles. The white brick Jan van Speijk Lighthouse stood at the center of the village. Corinne could hear the clip -clop of wooden klompen across the market square. She enjoyed watching the opportunistic gulls snatch food from the hands of unsuspecting people as they walked along the beach.

Corinne and Gari took a carriage to their home at Schoolstraat Nummer 8 in the village of Egmondse aan Zee. The house was a simple structure in cream-colored stucco with a central chimney and a high-pitched roof covered in red slate shingles. Although the house was beautiful, it was an enormous step down from Corinne's family home in Baltimore. The simple kitchen had a sink with a drainboard on each side. There was a small table with four wooden chairs. Open shelving held a few dishes, white plates, and bowls and cups with a blue, green and red floral pattern on them. There was an icebox and a wood stove.

"I've hired a local girl to serve as a maid to help you out here," Gari said, when he noticed the look of dismay on Corinne's face.

The girl, not much younger than Corinne, approached from the kitchen side door and curtsied.

"Corinne, this is Anna. Besides taking care of the house, she sometimes models for me," Gari said.

"Pleased to meet you, Mevrau Melchers," Anna said. Anna had long, braided blonde hair and blue eyes.

"I don't know how I'll have time to paint and keep up a home," Corinne said.

"I had doubts as to whether you could adjust to life here," Gari said, as if he expected Corinne to argue.

"I appreciate your concern, dear, but I want you to know that I have the determination to succeed here. I hope that you continue to believe in me." Corinne paused before continuing, "and I would like to see the school now."

Gari and Corinne made their way to the school, with Corinne following slightly behind her husband. He was so familiar with the terrain. She struggled to keep up with him, finding that she had to take several steps to account for each one of his. The building was set back from the street and although it was a similar style to the other buildings in the village, the bricks were painted white instead of brown. The multi-paned picture windows added a welcoming touch to the building. Shutters painted with red triangles and points that touched at the center of each shutter adorned the windows. A wrought-iron weathervane cross twisted above the chimney. Above the door was a simple plaque engraved with the words "Waar en Klaar": *True and Clear.*

The charming exterior hinted to Corinne of what she would find inside. They passed through the red door and inside the studio space was a group of about thirty easels. The artists sat behind their easels, most of them were young women; only two of the painters were men. As she gazed at the student works mounted on the walls, Corinne noticed Vermeer was the Old Master influencer for the painters in this school.

"Attention, students," Gari commanded. "I would like to introduce my new wife, Corinne Melchers. She will join us as a student here."

A chorus of "Hois!" greeted Corinne.

"Would you like to paint a little right now?" Gari asked her.

"I would like that. But I don't want to copy the Vermeer. I'd like to paint a still life."

"I'll set one up for you, my dear."

Corinne settled on the stool behind the easel closest to her. As her teacher, Gari squeezed out some oil colors onto a palette and brought it to her. The easel already had a small wood panel on it. Only a few of the women began painting from the new still life that Gari had set up in the middle of the room. Gari began walking around the room, giving critiques as he passed each easel.

Corinne noticed she was having difficulty guiding the colors on her panel. They were running into each other and becoming muddy. Not what she wanted to happen. The paint on her panel was already too thick. Undoubtedly, these were the consequences of insufficient practice. She couldn't manipulate the paint and realized she may need to use the palette knife rather than her brush. She started another panel and laid down a thin layer of green. Then she mixed some lemon yellow, white, and cadmium red to create a thicker coat of pink that looked almost peach. It took one or two strokes, but she was making better progress. She cleaned her brushes repeatedly. Finally, her panel held a likeness to the peach-colored tulips of the still life in front of her.

Gari had made his way around the other students and was coming back to her.

"I love what you've done here," he exclaimed. "The colors are stunning."

Then he bent over and whispered in her ear, "I think I'm going to call you "Peachy" from now on."

Corinne blushed at his flirtations but winced internally. She thought as the creator and teacher of this art school, he would treat every artist as an equal. But now she wondered if he was somewhat exploitative of these students and if the women were only there to provide an income for him. She aimed to change that.

"How many female artists do you know?" she asked as they walked home from the school. "Do not say Mary Cassatt or Berthe Morisot."

"A few. Mostly the ones at the school here," Gari said.

"The problem is that this school will not offer these women the same opportunities as male artists. They'll always be at the bottom. Society will also pressure female artists to fulfill their homemaking duties first and create art second," Corinne said.

"And you're saying that women actually want to be artists," Gari said.

"Of course, they want to be artists. I want to be an artist. You knew that before you married me," she said. Inside she felt stretched to her limits, like a rubber band ready to snap.

Gari was silent for a while and the look on his face made Corinne think he was pondering what she had just said.

"I know it isn't fair for women. But you're here with me now. And with this school, we can make changes and make it better. It doesn't matter who the artist is if a painting is true and clear, like the sign says above the door." Corinne wasn't sure if Gari said this because he meant it or if he just wanted to get home from the school without an argument.

*

Corinne rarely saw her husband without a palette and paintbrushes in his hands. He was always painting. In the warmer months, Corinne liked to sit outside in their garden and read or do some needlework.

One afternoon, she looked up to see her husband setting up his easel in the garden.

When Corinne saw the finished painting later, she noticed that not only had he captured her doing her needlework, but he also captured their maid Anna with a watering can in her hand. Their rose arbor framed the central window of the house. As a married couple, they embraced the Dutch culture, and it showed in this painting, *The Unpretentious Garden.*

Corinne's first year as a newlywed passed quickly and soon it was Christmas time. Christmas was not celebrated with the same enthusiasm in Egmondse as it was in Corinne's house in Baltimore, so on Christmas Eve, Corinne jumped out of bed and called for Anna.

"Anna, you must run to the market and tell Kraakman the greenery merchant to bring me a tree. Just a very tiny tree. I'm going to decorate it and invite six or eight of Gari's models to come and see it," Corinne said.

"Yes, Ma'am," Anna said as she gathered her cloak and klompen.

Gari had already gone to the studio on the dunes. Corinne joined him after breakfast. They walked arm in arm back to the house.

"I heard from someone at the market that you made some purchases this morning," Gari said.

"Yes, I decided we need a small tree. Just to make this Christmas seem a little like the ones I had at home," Corinne said. Gari grunted in reply. Corinne thought he wasn't happy about her spending his money on something so frivolous.

When they crossed the canal to arrive at their house, Gari held the door for Corinne. When she walked in, she could hardly believe her eyes. In the center of the dining room was a tree that reached to the ceiling. Her mouth dropped at the sight of it.

"After you've decorated this tree, I believe the entire village should be invited to see it," Gari said. Corinne could hear the excitement in his voice.

"Each child shall have a toy, a cake, and a cup of chocolate," Corinne said. She still couldn't read her husband's moods. Sometimes he seemed so gruff, and yet his actions would then be so kind.

The next day, Christmas, Corinne went out to do her shopping. As she went from shop to shop, she invited the children to follow her home. By the time she arrived at home, she had assembled quite a large group of children after walking from the canal to the church.

"Wait here," she said to the children at the gate. Inside, she, Gari, and Anna decorated the tree with cakes, candies, cheap toys, tissue paper, and candles. They lit the candles and then opened the door.

The smallest children circled the tree to pick out a treasure. Anna had hot chocolate for each of them. The oldest children had to remain outside the house because there wasn't room for all of them, but Anna took hot chocolate outside for them as well. Corinne looked on as one little boy stuck his finger in his cup when the chocolate was finished and swirled his finger all around to get every last bit of it. Gari put his arm around his wife as she smiled at the children's cheerful faces. Tears glistened in Corinne's eyes.

"What a wonderful sight. I'm so glad we did this," Corinne said.

The next morning, as Corinne walked through the village, a small boy ran up to her and said, "Dank u Mevrau fu het mooi Koostbaum." *Thank you, Madam, for the beautiful Christmas tree.*

So much had happened to Corinne in one year's time. She was now Mrs. Gari Melchers, an artist. She thought to herself, *would the next year be as transformative and rich with opportunities as this one had been?*

Chapter 4

1904: The Paris Medal

The answer to Corinne's question came in January. They got the news that President Loubet of France had promoted Gari from the grade of chevalier to that of an officer of the Legion of Honor. He received the honor as other artists had, by exhibiting the flawless performance of his trade. Established by Napoleon Bonaparte, this honor was the highest decoration given by France. When the letter arrived, Gari couldn't wait to show it to Corinne.

"Corinne, we're going to Paris!" He waved the letter in excitement as if it was an invitation from a family member he hadn't seen in twenty years.

"Why are we going to Paris?" He had her attention.

"I have been promoted as an officer of the Legion of Honor. You already know that I was a chevalier after winning the Grand Prize at the Paris Expo with John Sargent. There will be a ceremony and a ball. George and Henrietta will join us. Do you have a suitable dress to wear?"

"I suppose I could wear one from our honeymoon trip last year," Corinne said.

"You don't seem very excited. This is a prestigious award," Gari said.

"I understand. But I have my own paintings now that I would like to be recognized for," Corinne said.

"That will come in time, my dear," Gari said. Even her rude response couldn't quell his excitement.

"I am happy for you truly. But can't you understand why this is difficult for me?"

Gari's excitement dimmed slightly as he studied his wife's face. "I thought we were in this together. My success is your success, and vice versa. Perhaps we can find a way for you to meet some influential people at the ceremony. It's about time the world saw your talent, too."

"That would be fine. And I suppose it will be nice to be in Paris in January. It is dreadfully cold here in the winter months. Paris won't have the chill wind from the North Sea, but it could possibly be snowing. How will that affect our travel plans?" Corinne asked.

"The city draped in snow, the quiet streets, the way the light reflects off the Seine in winter. It could be incredibly inspiring for your work. Why don't you bring your sketchbook? You could capture Paris in a way few have seen it."

"That's actually a wonderful idea," Corinne admitted. Her enthusiasm was growing.

The next afternoon, Corinne rode her bike to George and Henrietta's house in Egmondse aan den Hoef.

"Hello, Corinne!" Henrietta answered the door with a smile on her face at this unexpected visit. "Come into the kitchen and let's have a cup of tea."

They sat down at the small wooden table in the kitchen. Corinne blew on her hands to warm them. Henrietta could see the look of concern on Corinne's face.

"What's troubling you, dear?" She asked.

"Henrietta, you've been married to George for some time now. Is this what it's always going to be like? Traveling to receive awards and going to exhibits?" Corinne asked.

"Well, that's the hope. And why don't you call me Miggles? Everyone else does. The awards and the exhibits pay the bills," Henrietta said matter-of-factly.

"But don't you want more for yourself? Is the art world only for men who are comfortably situated?"

"Most of the curators who are running museums are men. Men are the art buyers for galleries. Men are given most of the opportunities. You went to art school. You know this," Henrietta said.

"I know Gari is a good man. And he makes wonderful paintings. I just want more for myself."

"You have talent. What's meant for you won't pass by you," Henrietta said. She patted Corinne's hand.

The Melchers and the Hitchcocks traveled to Paris together. They stepped from the train at the Gare du Nord onto the platform. It was a change from their quaint fishing village into the working-class crowds of Parisians in the station. People rushed by them, and Corinne caught snippets of conversations as they passed.

Gari flagged down a carriage. "We'll be going to L'Hotel, Rue des Beaux Arts."

They passed by dozens of cafes and stores with pretty awnings on both sides of the street. The cafes had small tables and chairs set up for two people on the sidewalks. Waiters in long black aprons whisked small cups of coffee to the tables.

"After we're settled in the hotel and we get through the ball, I want to show my studio to you. It's close to here," Gari said to Corinne in the carriage, interrupting her sightseeing.

"I'm sure it's lovely, but I can't help feeling a bit envious," Corinne said, forcing a smile.

"You can share the space with me while you're here," Gari offered.

"It's not just about having space. It's about recognition, about being seen as an artist in my own right. Not just as your wife," Corinne said.

"I see. I guess I hadn't realized how much this meant to you," Gari said.

"I do want to see your studio. Just be patient with me if I'm a little quiet about it," Corinne said.

Gari nodded slowly.

Soon the evening of the ball arrived. In the hotel room, Henrietta and Corinne laced each other's corsets, each leaning against the bedpost. Corinne's back already ached as the corset attempted to mold her lower back to arch into an S-shape. They donned white, frilly ballgowns.

"I love to dance, Miggles, but I'm not sure dressing like this is worth it," Corinne laughed.

Gari and George were waiting in the hotel lobby for their wives. Gari gasped as Corinne came down the staircase. Her auburn hair was pulled into an updo. She floated down the stairs in her white dress with a fan next to her face. He was never tired of looking at his beautiful, young wife.

When they entered the ballroom, the first order of business was for the recipients to be awarded their medals. The crowd looked on as President Loubet pinned the distinctive blue ribbon with the gold cross onto Gari's lapel, and Gari shook his hand. The president then moved on to pin a medal onto John Singer Sargent's lapel. Once each artist received his medal, the crowd erupted in applause.

Afterwards, Gari joined Corinne on the ballroom floor. Corinne found herself following her husband around like a puppy, and she didn't like it. As Gari had been through a similar ceremony when he became a chevalier, he knew many of the guests.

"Let me introduce you to Guillaume Appolinaire," Gari said as he shook hands with the poet. "Mssr. Appolinaire, this is my wife, Corinne."

"Pleased to meet you," Corinne curtsied and fanned her neck.

"Enchantée," Guillaume said as they exchanged kisses on the cheeks.

"Corinne, Mssr. Appolinaire is a poet," Gari said.

"I understand you are one of the honored guests this evening for your artwork," Guillaume said to Gari. "You must meet my new friend, Pablo Picasso, from Spain. He is doing some very interesting painting right now."

"I would love to meet him, but I'm not sure we share the same outlook on art," Gari said. "Would you excuse us right now? There is someone I must talk to."

Gari and Corinne moved on to the next circle of attendants. A short woman with dark-framed glasses that circled her eyes was speaking to a few gentlemen.

"Madam Weill, it's so nice to see you here," Gari said. "I'd like to introduce you to my wife, Corinne. Corinne, this is Berthe Weill. She is an art dealer here in Paris."

"Pleased to meet you, Madame Weill," Corinne said. Meeting a female art dealer was an unexpected surprise of the evening.

"Please, call me Berthe," Berthe said, as they embraced.

"My wife has been doing some painting you may be interested in," Gari said.

"I've been looking at a few of the artists who are painting in a new style where their subjects are broken up and painted from many different viewpoints simultaneously. Picasso has been doing this kind of painting. I find it so interesting," Berthe said.

"I paint nothing like that . . ." Corinne began to explain her style.

Gari barely listened to her as he was looking over the tops of heads, searching through the crowd for the next person he wanted to talk to. It wasn't long before he was taking Corinne by the elbow and pushing her toward the next crowd of people.

"Please excuse us," Gari said.

"But I wasn't finished speaking to Berthe!" Corinne whispered sternly so that only Gari could hear her.

"We'll be right back," Gari said.

Gari escorted Corinne to the bar, and they each accepted a flute of champagne. Gari scanned the lively mix of guests at the bar and spotted a familiar face.

"John!" he said, as he slapped the back of another man standing at the bar. "You remember my wife, Corinne?"

"I don't think I've met your wife yet, Gari," John said. He reached to kiss Corinne's gloved hand.

"I've heard all about you, Mr. Sargent. Congratulations on winning this extraordinary honor. I know that you and my husband have been painting and exhibiting together for years," Corinne said.

"You have been hiding this beautiful woman. She'd make quite a model," John said.

"I'm keeping her for myself, and I don't think I want to share her," Gari said, playfully.

"Please excuse us, John. I see that Mr. Herrick, the American ambassador, has just arrived," Gari said. He put his hand on the small of Corinne's back and steered her to yet another corner of the ballroom.

"I don't see the point of trying to talk to people if you push us onto the next conversation before the earlier one is even finished," Corinne said.

"Here, it's just a matter of being seen," Gari said. "They will never remember our conversations."

Soon the band was playing some lovely waltzes. Corinne and Gari floated around the dance floor.

"You look absolutely stunning this evening. I find myself falling more in love with you each day," Gari whispered into Corinne's ear.

"I love you, too," Corinne said, sincerely. She could never stay angry at her husband for long.

Corinne was relieved when the night was over, and she was back in her hotel room. She could hardly wait to shed her corset. Waking up beside her husband the next morning was a sweet transition from the frenzied evening. She loved seeing his tousled hair against the pillow.

*

A few mornings later Gari took Corinne to see his Paris studio on the lower slopes of Montparnasse. They walked through the grayish-blue doors, and right away Corinne faced one of Gari's massive old easels, spotted with paint. The glass ceiling and sunshade cast shadows in the room. The wooden floor creaked as she walked across it. An old wood stove with exposed pipes warmed the room from the corner.

As Gari painted at his Paris studio throughout the spring, Corinne took the opportunity to explore Paris. At the boulangerie each morning, she bought a baguette and tucked it under her arm just as she saw the Parisians do. She enjoyed watching the people promenading up and down the avenues and through the manicured gardens. Some boys played a stick and hoop game next to her on the gravel walkway and she had to sidestep them so that she didn't interfere with their game. One day she read in the newspaper that an odd couple was on display at the Paris Zoo: an African Lion was mated with an Indian Tiger and had produced two baby hybrids. In their fur colorings, the male cub resembled his mother, and the female took after the father. Corinne stood watching them in their cage for hours.

In the past year, Gari and Corinne had talked about almost everything. The only thing they hadn't discussed was having a family, but privately, even when she saw baby animals, the thought came to her mind. They both were keenly aware that Corinne had not conceived, but it seemed a taboo topic to discuss out loud.

*

As they had missed Queen's Day the year before, Corinne was eager to return to Egmondse at the end of April to join in with the festivities. The couple traveled by train back to the coast. While in Paris, she had purchased an orange linen dress with a flowing jacket to wear on the celebratory day. In Holland, everyone wore orange on Queen's Day. The royal family was from the House of Orange, and thus orange was everywhere in a salute to the national color. The town vibrated with the carnival atmosphere and became one giant party. It was a day for the entire country to celebrate the royal family.

Corinne took Gari's arm as they walked along the Egmondse main street to the bakery. They ogled the tompouce in the window, two puffs of pastry with light orange cream in the middle and bright orange on the top. They went inside and bought some for breakfast. Corinne laughed as she and Gari tried to eat the difficult pastry without smearing it on their clothes.

Gari explained to Corinne that this day was the perfect day to look through the free markets to find knick-knacks to use in their still lifes. Queen's Day was the one day of the year that everyone was permitted to sell items with no permits. The whole country became a large flea market. People had thrown blankets and rugs down in front of their homes and spread out their offerings. The couple stopped to listen to a group of children singing Dutch songs in the street. It was a brilliant performance.

"This is such a fun day, but I'm afraid I'm going to go home empty-handed from the sales," Corinne said as she hummed along to the children's song.

"Look at this, Corinne!" Gari exclaimed as he held up an embossed, cream-colored Wedgwood soup tureen. "No chips or cracks."

"Finally, we've found something! That will be a lovely centerpiece for our table and something interesting to paint, too. Let's take it home," Corinne said.

*

Summer turned to fall, and one day, Gari called to Corinne as he saw her walk past the studio door with a palette in her hand.

"Peachy, I'd like you to start modeling for me. With your blue eyes and fair complexion, you can certainly pass for a Dutch girl. Try on this green dress and headdress."

Corinne agreed reluctantly, even though she herself had been headed outside to paint. Corinne slipped off her work clothes, and

Gari helped her pull the green dress over her head. After he buttoned up the back, he twirled Corinne around and held her hands in his. She wrapped her fingers around his and reveled in the feel of his hands against hers. So many wonderful works of art had come from those hands.

As the days went on, Corinne stood still for hours in a corner of the studio, posing. A white cap decorated with pink roses was tied tightly under her chin. She longed to be outside painting in the golden fall sunlight. To make matters worse, Gari sometimes spent an hour looking at his newspaper before beginning to paint. But if Corinne didn't show up and stand where he wanted her, he yelled belligerently. She loved his genius but didn't love his temper.

As he called her Peachy, Corinne took to calling him, "Mr. M."

"I could be doing my own painting rather than standing here for an hour while you get ready, Mr. M," Corinne said. "Or I could be modeling for John Singer Sargent."

Gari grunted from behind his paper. Then he began gathering his paints and brushes.

"I cannot paint you with a frown on your face," Gari said.

In the end, the painting became *La Brabanconne.* The title carried two meanings, as it was the name of the Belgian National Anthem, as well as the French term for a young, Belgian woman. Gari completed the painting with a small gray cat at the hem of Corinne's dress. Corinne didn't argue with the title, but Gari had told her she could pass for a Dutch girl when she began modeling for him. Gari propped the large painting in a corner of the classroom.

"I'm looking forward to showing this painting to George to see what he thinks of it. I know that George likes using the locals as models. But I'd like to hear what he thinks of you as my Dutch model," Gari said. As if on cue, there was a knock at the door, and when Corinne opened it, there stood George.

Chapter 5

1905: Best Friends' Divorce

George Hitchcock floated in and out of their little art school by the sea. They never knew for sure when they would see him. Gari taught a class on color theory. Corinne joined the other students one morning and listened intently as Gari described how to use color as a means of expression. The class was interrupted when George knocked on the doorjamb and entered the room with a new student by his side. She was a striking young woman in a purple dress with a white collar.

"One may teach drawing by a universal rule, but the same is not true for color," Gari explained to the class.

"Gari, excuse my interruption, but I have a new student for you," George said. "May I introduce Cecil Jay." Cecil's smile lit up the room.

"Good morning, Miss Jay," Gari said. "I was discussing color theory with the class."

"Good morning, Mr. Melchers," Cecil said. "George has been telling me all about you."

"I met Cecil in London, and I whisked her away from there," said George. "She paints watercolor miniatures, and I told her she must come and paint them on the Dutch seaside."

"Let me finish my class and we can discuss this more later. Why don't you take Cecil to our house and wait for us there," Gari said.

Corinne frowned as she noticed George steer Cecil out of the room with his hand on the small of her back.

After class, Gari and Corinne returned home to find George and Cecil, sitting snugly on the sofa. The maid, Anna, had served them some coffee and ontbijtkoek while they waited. They were so involved in their conversation that they didn't seem to hear Gari and Corinne enter the room. Gari cleared his throat.

"There you are," George was beaming. "Sorry to interrupt your class this morning, but I couldn't wait for you and Cecil to meet."

"This is my wife, Corinne," Gari said to Cecil.

"I can assure you that I've studied art at the Royal Academy in London, and I've had some of my miniatures exhibited there. I won't hold up your classes by needing special instruction. But George tells me the light and color of the Dutch seaside will improve my miniatures. So here I am," Cecil said.

"You're welcome to attend the classes at the school. Or to paint on your own with personal help from George or me," Gari said.

"George thinks I should do some miniature genre paintings with Dutch themes," Cecil said.

"Yes, when she finishes her series, we're going to go on tour together," George said.

"I think the Dutch miniatures sound lovely," Corinne replied as politely as she could. She was thinking of Henrietta— her best friend and George's wife.

"You're a painter, as well?" Cecil asked Corinne.

"Yes, I've been painting for a few years now," Corinne said.

"Where have you exhibited?" Cecil asked.

"I submitted some work to the Salon a few years ago, but they were rejected. I thought I would try again after painting here in Egmondse. It is an inspirational place to paint," Corinne acknowledged.

They continued to talk about the art school and how Cecil could benefit from involvement with it. Soon afterwards, George and Cecil left together. As Gari closed the door behind them, he and Corinne looked at each other in disbelief.

"What is going on?" Corinne asked.

"You know George," Gari said. "I'm sure it's just a fling and won't amount to anything. He flirts with everyone."

"This looks a little more serious than just a flirtation," Corinne said. "I'm concerned."

Only a few months after that, Corinne sat next to Henrietta as she laid her head on her hands on her kitchen table at the house in Egmondse aan den Hoef. Henrietta wept and tried to get the words out.

"George left me for his twenty-two-year-old student, Cecil Jay," Henrietta said.

"I'm so sorry for what you are going through," Corinne said as she rubbed Henrietta's back. "I'm here for any support you need of me."

"They're moving to Paris," Henrietta sobbed. "He wants a divorce. We've been married for twenty-five years and have children! I knew he always had girlfriends, but I never thought he would leave."

"I don't know about his other girlfriends, but I have met Cecil. He's still going to support you and the children even if you're divorced, isn't he?"

"Yes, he will support me but that doesn't make it feel any better."

"You can't stay in a relationship if the other person's heart isn't there. You can't make him love you by loving him harder," Corinne said.

"I know," Henrietta sobbed.

"You're strong and we'll get through this together," Corinne said.

Corinne wanted to offer comfort and support to her friend, but she had no personal experience to draw from. It was also difficult for her because George was one of Gari's best friends.

Henrietta lifted her head. Her eyes were red and swollen from crying. Corinne poured each of them a cup of tea.

"I'm used to being alone," Henrietta sniffled as she wiped her nose and then sipped her tea. "He always travels for exhibits and shows. I'm used to the long hours he spends away and how consumed he is by his work. I just never knew that he wanted to be with another artist. Gari was smart in marrying you. He'll never leave you because you understand him. Gari sees you as a partner in life and in art."

"This isn't about me," Corinne said to her friend. "I care about you and I'm here for you. I admire your immense courage. Whatever you need."

"Thank you," Henrietta said. "Your friendship means the world to me."

A few weeks later, Henrietta showed Corinne a letter of sale for the house at Egmondse aan den Hoef. She was nothing like the weeping mess she had been before. She was standing tall in a lightweight, ruffled white dress with puffed sleeves above the elbow. Her auburn hair, with a touch of gray, was full and wavy. She exuded confidence that maybe she didn't fully feel.

"I'm buying the house from George with help from Mr. Shannon," Henrietta said. "I'm going to stay in North Holland. This is our home."

James Shannon was another of their artist friends. He had painted a portrait of Gari several years prior that had been exhibited at the Paris Salon.

"James and his wife Florence have been very supportive of me," Henrietta continued. "I think Florence understands that I need to remain in Holland with my children."

"That's wonderful news, Miggles," Corinne said. "Gari and I will also help you in any way that we can."

"I can model for Gari at the school to make some money, if he wants me," Henrietta said. "I've done it before."

"Of course," Corinne said, as she grasped Henrietta's hand.

Corinne felt proud of Henrietta. Her friend was handling the situation with dignity. Corinne wasn't so sure that she could do the same if Gari left her for someone else.

*

Not long after this, during a walk through the market, Corinne and Gari noticed one of the wild game vendors shooing a dog away from his stand with a broom. The dog was a small retriever, white with brown patches. The dog cowered under the broom strikes and would crawl a few feet away, only to return a few minutes later.

"Why are you chasing that dog away?" Corinne asked.

"Haven't you heard about the hydrophobia?" The man asked her brusquely.

"No, I'm afraid I haven't."

"Recently a large brown dog came up to one of the police officers in the next village at three o'clock in the morning. The police officer thought nothing of it until the dog bit him severely. Others discussed with him the possibility of the dog being mad and the police officer still laughed it off. He said he was not afraid, and he would take his chances. Within a short time, the man was taken ill with symptoms of hydrophobia, and he died after dreadful suffering," the man explained.

"What does that have to do with this dog? Isn't this your dog?" Corinne asked.

"I can't be taking any chances. I've got a whole farm full of animals and I've heard of whole herds of cattle dying from rabies," the man said.

"May I take him home with me?" Corinne asked. Gari shot her a dirty look. The man threw a rope to Gari so he could fashion a leash out of it.

"You'll be doing me a favor. But don't say I didn't warn you," the man said.

"Are you sure you want to do this?" Gari asked her. "What if he develops rabies?"

"What's to become of him otherwise?"

"I'm inclined to forbid it," Gari said. "We should not have animals living in our house."

Corinne ignored him and took the rope from his hands. "What's his name?" She asked the farmer.

"We call him Luek," the man said.

Corinne fastened the rope to the dog's collar. "Come along, Luek," she said.

Luek seemed happy to follow her and avoid the whacks from the broom. He didn't even look back. When she got back to the house, she warmed some milk and poured it into a bowl for him. Before long, she noticed Gari sitting next to Luek on the floor. Gari scratched behind his ears as he lapped up the milk.

"I guess you'll be some kind of guard dog," Gari said.

"He can also be a model for our paintings. And he'll stay in the house next to the hearth, so there will be no chance of him getting rabies," Corinne smiled to herself.

"Would you take him to the veterinary, too? Just to be sure he doesn't have rabies?" Gari asked.

"The veterinary? That would be quite expensive. Is that really necessary?" Corinne asked.

"It would put my mind at ease," Gari answered.

"Very well, I'll see to it as soon as possible," Corinne said.

Gari continued to paint everyday life in Holland. Modern women in beautiful interiors became a theme for him. He began a painting he titled *Open Door*. He used both Corinne and Henrietta as models and used the parlor of Henrietta's house at Schuylenburg as the setting. Corinne didn't mind this modeling, as she had her friend to talk with throughout the sitting— unlike the *La Brabaconne* painting, in which she had to stand still in the corner of the studio by herself.

The women sat around a table, featured in the background of the painting. Sunlight streamed into the room, and that part of the painting was full of light pastel colors. The cheerful interior, adorned with rose garland wallpaper, belied the fact that Gari could only use the parlor as the setting because his friend Hitchcock had abandoned his wife and home. Had Hitchcock still owned the house, Gari would never have had the chance to use it. In the darker hallway at the front of the painting, a servant waits on the two women to finish their conversation. The painting was a fusion of realism and impressionism.

"Next, I want to paint a standing portrait of you, Peachy," Gari said at breakfast one day.

"I suppose that means I'll be standing in the studio for hours and hours each day," Corinne said.

"We can take breaks as we need to," Gari said. "But you inspire me to paint."

"I would like to do some painting, too, Mr. M," Corinne said.

"You know what I told you on our wedding night? My artist friend Hopkinson Smith told me this: It takes two to paint a picture: one to paint it and that other fellow to hit him over the head with a club when it's time to stop. You'll have to be that other fellow for me. You make me a better artist," Gari said.

"I know you have an irresistible urge to paint," Corinne said. "You never tire of your craft. But I feel creativity calling to me, as well."

Corinne stood in one corner of the studio in a long, flowing white gown. She was beautiful, facing to the left, her right hand placed lightly atop her breast. Her left hand was by her side.

They discussed Gari's career as he painted.

"The problem with me is that I don't enjoy talking to the press. I close up like a clam when I'm confronted with art critics and reporters," Gari said. "And I don't want to talk about my friends, Sargent, Hitchcock, and Whistler. About how alike or how different we are."

"But you do talk about your affinity for Mary Cassatt's mother and child paintings," Corinne said.

"I admire her greatly," Gari said. "You know we worked on some murals together at the Chicago World's Fair."

"I would like to meet her someday," Corinne said.

"I think I should keep the two of you apart. Or you will leave me to paint with her in her studio," Gari said.

The devotion that Gari felt for his wife was manifest in the life-sized portrait of her when he completed it. He titled it simply *Portrait of My Wife.* Corinne was stunning in three-quarter profile, before a fairy tale backdrop. The painting expressed light in the Impressionist style, with pale colors, but Gari had retained a realistic handling of his model.

"I love it," Corinne admired the painting when it was finished.

The Detroit Museum of Arts invited Gari back to his hometown of Detroit for the opening of the auditorium in April. He took the painting of Corinne along and showed it at a reception given in his honor. The reception was held in the main hall on the second floor of the museum. The main hall already held one of his earlier works: *The Letter.* He was lauded as one of the ten great painters of the day, along with Whistler and Sargent, and this new painting of Corinne confirmed his place in the contemporary American art world.

Chapter 6

1907: INFERTILITY

In April, Corinne and Henrietta sat in the dining room enjoying tea. They had closely recreated the *Open Door* painting tableau that Gari had painted a few years before. Sunlight streamed through the open window. They could smell the sea. Henrietta had some news for her friend.

"I married Charles Lewis Hind in a simple civil ceremony. He's a wonderful man. I believe you and Gari will like him. He is a writer specializing in art history but also an artist himself. I hope you're not angry with me for marrying so quickly without telling you," Henrietta said.

"Miggles, I'm not angry. I'm so happy that you have someone new, and that you're happy!" Corinne said to her friend.

"It's ironic that I met him through George. He has written many critiques of George's paintings. He's known for helping the ordinary man enjoy and understand art. Charles inspires me to write, too, now that my children are grown. I've been around artists for years. I think I know them well enough to write about them," Henrietta said.

Corinne smiled.

"I also have a little bad news. I am moving to London to be with him. He has a house there. I'm afraid you and I won't be together anymore," Henrietta said.

Now it was Corinne's turn to cry. Tears welled up in her eyes before she could stop them.

"Don't cry. We'll write. And we'll see each other every so often," Henrietta said, as now it was her turn to console her friend.

"Charles has asked me to give a lecture on Gari's artwork in Detroit. They don't really know what to call me now. Mrs. Hitchcock Hind? Mrs. Lewis Hind? I plan to tell them that Gari Melchers and John Singer Sargent are the greatest American painters now that Whistler is dead. Gari's famous picture, *Mother and Child,* is a masterpiece," Henrietta said. She handed Corinne a pack of cards with her notes for her speech on them.

". . . so much human interest in that painting with the peasant mother holding the baby in her arms. All done in tones of brown except for the faces, arms, and child's white frock," Corinne read out loud from Henrietta's notes.

"I intend to show them that the colors make one feel the poverty and privation of their lives. He is realistically representing people as they were," Henrietta said.

"It is a most sensitive painting. Those who will disagree and criticize the most will likely be the least learned, and those who have experience observing art are more likely to applaud," Corinne said as she dried her tears. Discussing the talk distracted her from the fact that her best friend was moving away.

"Exactly. I hope I have more of the latter at my talk," Henrietta said.

With Henrietta gone and no one else in the house, Corinne taught herself to play scales on the piano; the activity made her hands tingle with comfortable warmth. It was about her fingers hitting the right keys at the right time. It was almost as enjoyable for her as painting.

Corinne played the piano whenever guests came to visit. She played harmony and melody using both hands. She tried to find joy in the process of playing instead of obtaining the goal of becoming a master piano player. It was incredibly empowering for her. She hoped she could take the lessons from learning to play the piano into her painting life. Learning the piano was a lifelong process and so was her painting. The tactile sensation of pressing the keys and producing beautiful melodies was such a source of joy for her.

One evening, shortly after she learned that Miggles was leaving, Gari announced that they would be traveling to Pittsburgh. The announcement halted Corinne's evening piano recital for her husband.

"Andrew Carnegie has built a beautiful art institute and will exhibit quite a few of my paintings in a founders' day ceremony. Including one of you. We'll be attending the dedication to the building," Gari said.

"Now that Miggles is gone, I'm looking forward to the trip. And perhaps we can visit my family on the way home. It will distract me," Corinne said.

"Luckily, we'll be missing the big flood that Pittsburgh had a month ago," Gari said. "Evidently, the rivers flood every year around this time with all the buildup of ice and snow."

A light springtime snow was falling as Gari and Corinne arrived, mid-morning, along with the other dignitaries, at the massive building in Schenley Park. A large automobile picked them up at their hotel and whisked them through the park. Corinne wrapped her neck in a fur scarf and stuffed her hands into a large fur muff to keep herself warm. Although Corinne enjoyed the novelty of the automobile ride, she coughed and choked from the sulfur smoke pouring out of the nearby steel mills.

Mayor Guthrie and his wife stepped out of their own automobile and walked to the large marble corridor next to Andrew Carnegie. Mr. Carnegie had a wide smile on his face.

"It's great. It's great," he repeated. He was a man of few words.

The group soon moved to the art galleries on the second and third floors. There were nine spacious rooms in all. The first thing that Corinne noticed were the number of portraits.

"It would take more than one day to inspect all these paintings. It does them a disservice to pass by them idly," Corinne whispered to Gari.

"The impressions will vary according to everyone's natural taste," Gari said.

"Could an artist ask for any greater tribute of praise than for someone to love a picture for what it means to them? Rather than the technical aspect of how it was painted?" Corinne asked.

Gari didn't respond but sauntered down the hallway with his hands clasped behind his back.

Upon entering the first gallery, Gari's work, a full-length portrait of a woman, dominated the end of the room. A woman, Mrs. H. D. Sheldon, posed in an ethereal gown accessorized with a black lace shawl. It had a Gainsborough-like background of woods, fields, and streams. It was a delight to look at this exquisitely gowned woman walking through the woods with her train sweeping the grass. There were two modest landscapes, one on each side of it, and their positioning made Mrs. Sheldon resemble a magical creature rather than just a portrait.

In the same gallery there was a picture of a young woman preparing the table for a meal. Gari had captured his Dutch colony's peasant life in this woman's dress, the food, and in the little corner of the room. A still picture of a girl was also there. Her expression suggested that she could speak, although she looked as if she was carved of stone.

A large canvas occupied the center of the next room. It was Gari's version of the Last Supper. Neither Gari nor Corinne were overtly religious, but Gari had captured the face of Christ and the light that radiated from him. The attention to the disciples, and their individualistic qualities, was a fascinating study.

Towards the gallery's exit, two of Gari's paintings stood out prominently, making it difficult for one to casually walk by. One was of a young mother holding her child against her shoulder. The picture was charming because there was so much love in the mother's face. But the portrait of Corinne was stunning. She was dressed in white satin with a rose scarf thrown about her head. Many of the guests gasped as they walked up to it.

"Such a woman may be capable of breaking hearts and equally capable of breaking her own," they overheard one man say.

It didn't escape Corinne's notice that Cecelia Beaux exhibited a whole room of portraits on the third floor. She remembered that Cecelia had been admitted to the Paris Salon in the year she herself had been rejected.

"Oh, to be her and have this entire room of my paintings. If only someone would say *yes* to my paintings," Corinne said to Gari as they walked through the gallery.

"Are you sure you want that confirmation? With it comes a lot of critique. Are you *really* sure you want the whole art world looking at your paintings?" Gari asked.

"Part of me craves that recognition, that validation. But then . . ."

"But then?" Gari asked.

"It's complicated. I want my art to be seen, to mean something to others. And then there's our life together . . ." Corinne said.

"What about our life?" Gari asked.

"Lately I've been dedicating myself to supporting your career. It's not a complaint; it's a choice I made. But sometimes I wonder if I've used that as an excuse, especially when I'm in a gallery of Cecelia's paintings, "Corinne said.

Gari took her hand. "You're more than capable, my dear."

"I know," Corinne said, squeezing his hand. "I just wish I could reconcile these parts of myself."

Corinne had a recurring dream while they were in Pittsburgh. She was climbing a ladder, higher and higher but could never reach the top. She was afraid of falling if she turned around to go back down. Henrietta's lecture on Gari's paintings, particularly the *Mother and Child* painting described as a masterpiece, haunted Corinne's thoughts. The painting mirrored her endless climb towards motherhood.

Corinne wanted to validate Gari's pain, to tell him he wasn't crazy for wanting a child so deeply that he painted them often. Internally, she felt alone and helpless, and she imagined that he felt similarly.

Corinne traveled from Pittsburgh to Baltimore to visit her mother and to consult a doctor about her fertility. Her mother arranged an appointment with the renowned gynecologist, Howard Kelly, at Johns Hopkins Hospital. After the examination, they discussed the results in his office.

"Dr. Kelly, do you know why I can't conceive?" Corinne asked. Most doctors believed that women who couldn't conceive were fragile and unstable. Corinne didn't feel this way.

"I believe there is a malposition of your uterus. It tilts backwards and it may be fixed to your pelvis," Dr. Kelly said.

"Is there anything you can do?"

"I will give you some exercises to do that may strengthen the ligaments and tendons that will hold the uterus in an upright position. You should try them first before we discuss surgical options," Dr. Kelly said.

"Thank you, Doctor. I'll try the exercises," Corinne said. Alone in the office, she wished Henrietta or her mother were there to hold her hand. She felt heartbroken over never being able to feel the love of a child or to give the love of a mother. Corinne yearned for a child to talk to while Gari was working. Corinne could hardly wait to return to Egmondse and turn her maternal energies into her garden, nurturing plants in place of children.

When she returned from the doctor's office, Gari was waiting for her.

"Every hour felt like two weeks since you've been gone. What did the doctor say?" he asked.

"He gave me some exercises to do and said there may be some surgical options. But I don't feel hopeful," Corinne said.

"I don't understand it, but we'll get through it together. I love you and I'll be at your side no matter what. We may have to accept that nature has other plans for us," Gari said.

Corinne smiled at her husband as she felt a tear roll down her cheek. He hugged her to his chest. She felt the coarse wool of his jacket coat against her cheek.

"You know my sister, Hettie, is one year older than me and my brother. Arthur is a few years younger. It was eleven years before my parents had another child after he was born. So, us older children played house with Julia as if she was our child rather than our sibling. I think my mother appreciated the help we gave her by taking Julia off her hands. Perhaps that experience will be enough for me, and we don't need a child of our own," Gari said, as he kissed the top of his wife's head.

Corinne wondered if childhood games would truly be enough.

Chapter 7

1908: The Presidential Portrait

"Peachy, we'll be leaving to go to my New York studio in February," Gari said as he sipped his coffee at the breakfast table.

"I don't fancy traveling across the Atlantic in February," Corinne said.

"I received a letter from Detroit. From Charles Lang Freer," Gari said. "The Detroit Museum of Art purchased the standing portrait of you. So, not only will we be going to New York to finalize that sale, we'll be stopping in Washington, DC. Mr. Freer will join us there."

"You are making this sound so intriguing," Corinne said. "Why are we stopping in Washington, DC?"

"We have been invited to lunch with the President of the United States," Gari said enthusiastically. "Mr. Freer owns many railroads and is also an art lover. He is working with the new Smithsonian Institution in Washington, DC. And after seeing the portrait I painted of you; he is commissioning me to paint a portrait of President Theodore Roosevelt."

"That is so exciting! I guess it paid off for me to stand for all those hours while you painted!" Corinne felt excitement for her husband, yet she simultaneously wished that they had asked her to paint the portrait. She loved her husband, but sometimes he was oblivious to her desire to paint.

They arrived at the White House on Friday, February 28th, the day after Corinne's birthday. Snow had transformed the White House into a winter wonderland. Corinne stepped out of the carriage, stopped short, and gazed at the immense columns in front of the mansion. She could hardly believe they were at the White House, a symbol of the country.

President Roosevelt enthusiastically greeted the couple in the Family Dining Room. Gari shook the president's hand and introduced himself. "Gari Melchers, Mr. President. And this is my wife, Corinne."

"What a pleasure to meet you both. My youngest sister's name is also Corinne. I believe it means 'beautiful maiden.' So fitting," President Roosevelt said, as he took Corinne's hand and led her to her seat.

"Thank you," Corinne said, blushing.

"Please, sit down. The staff has prepared this lovely lunch for us. After lunch, I'm going to put on my riding outfit," President Roosevelt said. "I thought we could discuss what I would wear. You can let me know what you think would look better in the painting."

"My wife often models for me and knows what fabrics and textures add depth and interest in a painting," Gari said. Again, Corinne thought to herself that she didn't want to be an assistant. She wanted to be the artist. But she decided to humor her husband.

"Black or brown boots?" President Roosevelt asked.

"Definitely brown," Corinne offered.

"Cravat and waistcoat colors?"

"Red cravat and deep, olive-green waistcoat. Besides the red cravat, let's include some yellow, as red and yellow are the colors of your regiment. All the details are important. In portraits, the value is greatly enhanced by the costume chosen and the way in which its material, coloring, and details are painted," Corinne said.

"I agree. With that all decided, you can meet me in this dining room again tomorrow morning at 9 a.m. sharp to make your preliminary sketches. This room has a north light," the president said.

When the president arrived to stand for the portrait the next day, he appeared as if he had just arrived from a day of hunting. He wore a black hunting jacket with a fur collar. In his left hand he held his leather gloves and a walking stick with a silver bird's head for a handle. His black Homberg added even more height. And his signature Pince-nez glasses gave him a look of sophistication.

Gari began by making a study of the pose that he wanted on a smaller canvas. Mr. Freer was present in the room as he started his work.

"I hope you don't mind if Mr. Freer and I conduct a little business while I'm posing," the president said.

"Not at all, Sir," Gari replied as he applied some paint to his palette.

"Mr. Freer, I understand you're undertaking a new museum in Washington DC," the president said, with hardly a change in his pose.

"Yes, Mr. President, I am donating my Japanese stoneware ceramics and tea ceremony items to the Smithsonian Institute," Freer said.

"We shall have a grand Japanese exhibition there," the president said.

"Mr. President, I'm also going to contribute funds to construct a building and an endowment to study Asian arts. I feel strongly that we should display these pieces in a city where tourists can see them. There will be over eight thousand pieces," Freer said.

"That's very generous of you," the president said.

"I have some requests, however. I would like to have full curatorial control over the collection while I'm alive. And I would like you to vouch for me as an expert in Asian arts," Freer said.

"I think you are very knowledgeable in all aspects of the Orient, and I will write a letter right away," the president said.

"Very good," Freer said. "I'll be on my way then."

He smiled and nodded to Gari as he left the room. Gari commented later to Corinne that he'd felt like a fly on the wall to be privy to this important conversation while painting.

*

On the second day of sketching and painting, Corinne sat in the corner of the room and observed her husband and the president.

"Are you getting tired? Do you want a rest?" Gari asked. The president had been standing for quite some time.

"No, no, no. Not at all," the president said.

"Aren't you tired yet? Maybe you want to shake your arms and legs out for a bit?" Gari asked, fifteen minutes later.

"Of course not."

"But you are doing far more than is required of professional models," Gari said.

"How much is that?" the president asked.

"I hold a pose for forty-five minutes and then relax for fifteen," Corinne said from the back of the room.

"Well, I'll double that," the president said with a wink in her direction.

The two men continued their conversation as Gari painted.

"Have you ever been to Asia?" the president asked of Gari.

"I have not. I have traveled all over Europe, but never Asia," Gari said.

"Tell me of some travels in Europe, then," the president said.

"Heavens! My friends and I had some ridiculous adventures in Italy. Nothing was too laughable or too undignified for us . . ." Gari paused to dab some paint on the canvas. "I remember pulling a refractory mule hitched to a vegetable cart for half a mile just by sheer force. The driver, an old woman, gave me fifteen sous, and we drank to one another's success at the next inn. Luck for one was luck for all in those merry days," Gari said. President Roosevelt laughed heartily, still managing to keep his pose.

*

Gari met with the president every day for a week to make his sketches. At the middle of the week, Corinne had been invited to do some sightseeing with Mrs. Roosevelt during the day. That evening, he filled her in on the sessions.

"He is a remarkable model. He never takes a rest. Stands for one or two hours without even moving," Gari said. "He is full of vigor, and as you have seen, we talk about all kinds of subjects."

"While you were painting, Mrs. Roosevelt and I went to see the Washington Monument. It is brilliant white and towers over the city. We went inside and took an elevator to the top. Do you know how long it took us to get to the top?" Corinne asked.

"How long?"

"Only seven minutes! It was quite exciting! And from the top we had panoramic views of the whole city," Corinne spoke rapidly.

"Sounds like a marvel of engineering. Perhaps I will have time to see it when I'm finished with the painting."

When the sketches were complete, Gari began working with charcoal on the large canvas. He chose a vast, four by seven-foot canvas and retrieved his brushes and paints. Gari sketched the president's face repeatedly as he felt he was not capturing the president's expression perfectly.

Everyone in the White House crowded around to watch him paint. Mrs. Roosevelt and her sister watched for some time. The president's young son, Quentin, often stole Gari's paint tubes, and his mother reprimanded him.

"You must be anxious, Mr. Melchers, to get this painting done in two weeks, and it isn't helping when Quentin steals your paints," Mrs. Roosevelt said.

"Look at what he does with them." Gari smiled as he pointed to some paintings of butterflies around his feet. "I cannot be anxious when I have a new artist in the making."

The president heard them talking as he was walking by the room.

"Don't hurry, Mr. Melchers. But you know, I feel you have made my face too round. Mrs. Roosevelt has scolded me for making you feel too hurried. This portrait is too important, and I will give you two sittings more so we can work on it," the president said.

Near the end of the two weeks as Gari was finishing the portion of the painting with the president's face, the president walked by him again.

"Dominant expression you're getting there, Mr. Melchers. It is really a different picture. That is the face of the man that sent the fleet across the world," the president said. *Finally, he's gotten it right,* Corinne thought to herself as she again watched Gari work from the corner of the room.

Gari finished the painting in the middle of March after only a few weeks of work. He and Corinne had breakfast at the New Willard Hotel on their final day and made plans to visit her family in Baltimore.

*

At her mother's breakfast table, Corinne reflected on how it had been eight years since she sat in her seat. Her mother still kept a vase of flowers on the table, and Corinne mapped out a still life of the flowers in her mind. She noticed again how the light hit everything on the table.

"How are things going with your marriage, Corinne? The measure of a woman is how well she marries," Louise said.

"Mother, the marriage is going well. But you know I want to be a successful artist more than I want to be a wife," Corinne said. Her mother laughed.

"Your husband painted a portrait of the President of the United States! I think you're a wife first and a painter second. Everything you do from now on will be in your husband's name."

Corinne busied herself with her soft-boiled egg. "It's important to me. Why can't you understand that?"

Soon, Gari joined them at the table. "How is my Peachy this morning?" He asked as he pecked her cheek with a kiss.

"I'm fine," Corinne answered. Gari didn't notice that she didn't seem to mean it.

Before they had a chance to leave Baltimore to return to New York, Corinne came down with the flu. She woke up weak, drifting in and out of consciousness one foggy morning. Her hands felt like ice, and although she was covered by a heavy quilt, she couldn't get warm.

"You probably shouldn't have been outside in the snow at the White House. It was too much for you," Gari said. "I'm calling for a doctor."

When the doctor arrived, Gari spoke to him. "She has a fever and a nasty cough."

Gari left the room to let the doctor examine her and to let Louise know what was happening.

"She'll recover quickly. It's just a spring cold," Louise said.

They both stood at the bottom of the stairs as the doctor came down. His brows were furrowed as he said, "Mrs. Melchers has severe congestion. If she does not stay warm and quiet, it will turn into pneumonia. It is a very grave illness. I recommend fluids and complete bed rest for several weeks. You should probably hire a night nurse for her."

"I'll look after her at night," Louise said. She closed her eyes and worried about her daughter sinking into worse health.

The next day, Corinne reached a thin hand out from under the covers to drink her tea and sip her soup. Gari sat in an armchair in the corner of the room with her. She had a coughing fit, and he jumped up to offer her some water to drink. He didn't stay long because he could see her energy was fading. She closed her eyes and slept.

After a week, a little more color returned to her face. She got up for an hour at a time and sat by the fire. She enjoyed having her mother there to fuss over her while she was sick. Gari didn't have his paints in Baltimore, so he spent his days sketching in his sketchbook.

"I think you are on the mend," Louise said to her as she came into the bedroom.

"I think so, too. I think my constitution is stronger than anyone has given me credit for. Thank you, Mother, for taking care of me," Corinne said. She sat with her mother's cat in her lap and stroked along its back; she listened to everyone coming and going in the house throughout the day. The severity of her illness brought her to ponder her life choices. Maybe her mother was right about being a wife first and a painter second. Her mother had been beside herself with worry. Maybe being a good wife was all that she should strive for, Corinne thought about her life as she adjusted the covers around herself on the bed.

Gari was relieved when Corinne was well enough that they could board the train to go to New York. He felt his wife's shoulder blade through the back of her coat and realized she had lost more weight with her illness than he thought. He vowed to himself to help her take it easy when they returned to their apartment.

Corinne happened to be the first to the mailbox and retrieved the note with the President's official seal after they had been in New York for a week. She could hardly wait for Gari to open it. She went to his studio and caught sight of him from the doorway. He was flushed, eager, gazing upon his work. There was a look on his face of happiness, exhilaration, and purpose. He was face to face with his art and all its possibilities of triumph or failure. He was never flippant about his work. Now that she had recovered from the flu, she couldn't help but run to him.

"An envelope from the White House!" she exclaimed. "Open it!"

Gari slit the top of the envelope with a letter opener. He slowly unfolded the letter inside.

> Dear Mr. Melchers,
>
> I am delighted with the picture and especially pleased that it was done by an American artist.
>
> Sincerely,
>
> President Theodore Roosevelt, Jr.

A few weeks later they also got a letter from Mr. Freer with a check for $2500.

> Dear Mr. Melchers,
>
> I am pleased with the portrait of President Theodore Roosevelt, Jr. You captured the dignity, force, and character of the president. It will hang in our new Asian museum.
>
> Art is a language, and your portrait will talk to the people through the coming centuries.
>
> Sincerely,
>
> Charles Lang Freer

Chapter 8

1909: The Weimar School

"I have been appointed as Director and Professor of Art at the Grand Ducal Saxony School of Art in Weimar, Germany," Gari folded up the letter he had received in the mail. "The school specializes in educating painters and sculptors. I could make such a difference there."

"So, we're moving to Germany?" Corinne asked. They had never discussed this possibility.

"Nature will inspire our paintings, and we'll do many landscape paintings in such a beautiful area of Germany. The hills are covered with pine forests that are so thick, they're always cool and dark, even in the brightest sunshine. Bubbling streams run into lovely valleys. I went to live in Germany when I was only seventeen. I studied under the great painter von Gebhardt in Dusseldorf. You'll love Germany just as much as you love Holland," Gari answered.

You've had so many more opportunities with your painting than I have had, Corinne thought to herself.

"Before we leave, I want to capture the beauty of the beach here. There's a full moon tonight," Corinne said. She gathered her easel and paints and made her way to the dunes. At first, the sky turned a dusty blue and then faded into pink. Then the moon lifted high above the dunes, and Corinne painted furiously, trying to capture the luminous glow, the swirl of dark sky, and the wisps of clouds around it.

Gari walked up behind her. His arms encircled her waist.

"I don't want to forget this. I've loved our life here. Living here next to the sea," Corinne said.

"We can return here whenever we want. We'll always have the school," Gari said.

When they arrived in Weimar in the summer, Corinne saw how the Arts and Crafts style school building and the Art Nouveau were so different from their studio in Holland on the seaweed-strewn beach. The skylight hall and elliptical staircase in the Art Nouveau studio were especially lighter and brighter. The studio faced Franz Liszt's old home. There was a park close by with many walking trails where she could sketch or paint outside.

Corinne made an oil painting of the interior of their new home. The white door opened onto a lovely parlor. There was a frieze of red and white wallpaper around the top of the room with matching scarlet drapes. A brown sofa sat under a portrait of Gari's. Several red patterned Oriental rugs were on the floor. Opposite each other were green and blue sitting chairs, all waiting for visitors to sit in them for conversation. Corinne was able to give this painting the illusion of space so others could feel just as she did when she opened the door to that room. As Corinne painted, she thought to herself of how much she loved all the homes she had lived in throughout her life.

Corinne enjoyed hanging a basket over her arm and going to the market in the morning. There was always an old Romani man dragging an organ with a small monkey perched on top of the instrument. The monkey wore a red jacket and pants with a gold braid, and the pants had a small hole so his tail could stick through. Corinne would give the monkey a coin and a small piece of apple or pear just to see the monkey tip his hat to her. She felt like she and the monkey shared a secret when they smiled at each other.

"Don't you mistreat that monkey," Corinne said to the old man as she also handed a coin to him. The man nodded and tipped his hat, although he probably didn't understand what she was saying.

Gari was painting an evening church scene that he titled *Easter Sunday* from some of his sketches from Egmondse aan den Hoef. With thick layers of paint, he captured the sunlight streaming through the stained-glass windows. The scene depicted the Dutch village women attending the prayer service. At the canvas' base, they seemed to sit on the frame.

"It was you who told me there would be so many things to paint here in Germany, and yet you continue to paint Dutch scenes," Corinne said when she saw the finished painting.

"Maybe I'm a little homesick for the Dutch seaside," Gari said.

As fall came, Corinne looked forward to celebrating St. Martin's Tag in Weimar. The children in the town dressed up in costumes, carried lanterns, and followed a man on horseback dressed as St. Martin. Corinne could hear them singing as they walked past her house. Red and yellow leaves crunched under her boots as she stepped outside to give them some candy as they passed. In the town square there was a massive bonfire, and the townspeople gave the children pretzels. She had her maid cook a large goose with red cabbage and dumplings.

As they watched the children going from house to house, Gari said, "I wanted us to have a family someday."

"I would like that, too. But given that we haven't conceived a child yet and with what the doctor said, I think we have to accept that is not going to happen," Corinne said. "We have Luek."

Gari leaned over and kissed her. Relief flooded Corinne's face. She scratched behind Luek's ears as he looked up adoringly at her face. Luek was an old dog now, and his muzzle sparkled with gray hairs.

Because Corinne was married to the art director, she frequently ran into Emma von Schirach, who was married to the director of the Weimar Court Theatre, Carl von Schirach. Both Carl and Emma were from Philadelphia. At thirty-seven, Emma was closer to Corinne's age than most of their other friends.

Corinne invited them to have Thanksgiving dinner at the Melchers' home. She directed her housekeeper to cook a dinner complete with turkey, dressing, sweet potatoes, and cranberries. When they walked in the door, the von Schirachs inhaled the scents of the sage and cinnamon. On the sideboard were pumpkin, mince, and apple pies.

"Please come in and sit down," Corinne said. She was wearing a maroon dinner dress with bronze cuffs and collar.

Gari sat at the head of the table and said grace. The dinner discussion turned to their similar, yet different, backgrounds.

"How did you ever end up in Germany when you both were born in Philadelphia?" Corinne asked.

"We have a German heritage and have some ties to this region. My father was Karl Friedrich von Schirach. He was a major in the US Civil War on the Union side and in the honor guard for Abraham Lincoln's funeral. You know, it was Abraham Lincoln who proclaimed Thanksgiving as a national holiday," Carl said.

"I guess we were on opposing sides of the war, then," Corinne said. Corinne bristled at mention of the war. "Both my father and my grandfather fought for the Confederacy. The North destroyed the South during the war, but the men who fought were brave men. They were the bravest of the brave. I felt Lincoln was never my president."

"We all wanted reconciliation for our country after the war," Emma said. "We could ask the same question of you; how did you end up in Germany?"

"The Grand Duke invited Gari to teach painting here. I had just become accustomed to life on the Dutch coast and then we moved here so that Gari could take up this post. I grew up in the Southern United States, though. I spent some time in Savannah and Baltimore," Corinne said.

"Your roots grow deep," Emma said.

"I am a daughter of the Confederacy," Corinne said. "I believe we needed to care for the widows and children of the dead Confederate soldiers."

"This is probably not suitable talk for ladies at the dinner table," Gari gruffly said. He pulled his shoulders back and sat up straighter in his chair. Corinne shot him a glaring look. Gari was a young child in Michigan during the Civil War and left at seventeen for Europe. He didn't share Corinne's enthusiasm for the Confederacy.

"Emma and I will take our coffee in the parlor," Corinne said, and she and Emma left the dining table to continue their discussion.

"This is a day to be thankful, and I'm thankful that I have you for a friend here in Germany," Corinne said.

"I appreciate all that we have here in Weimar," Emma said. "I get the sense that you're not entirely happy here. What do you do to occupy your time?"

"I paint, play the piano, do some embroidery," Corinne said.

"What do you paint?"

"I've painted still lifes, landscapes, portraits . . . I graduated from the Maryland School for the Arts."

Corinne walked over to the painting on the wall and pointed to it. It was the painting she had done of the interior of her new home.

"I painted this," she said.

"That is marvelous! I was certain that was one of Gari's paintings! Do you exhibit these anywhere?" Emma asked.

"I haven't, but I would like to."

"The Brücke is a group of German artists trying to link past, present and future. They do a more graphic style, but perhaps you could exhibit with them. Carl is a friend of the director of the Kunsthall Mannheim. He is trying to expand the museum and have a German art exhibit of American painters next year. Shall I tell him you're interested?"

"Yes, tell him that I have many paintings to show him," Corinne said excitedly. She stood up and retrieved the von Schirachs' coats from the closet. Emma took the coats, met her husband in the dining room, and departed from the Melchers' home.

*

The calendar turned from November to December, and Corinne asked Gari if they could return to Egmondse aan Zee for Christmas. She liked her new friend Emma, but she missed Miggles too. They booked a room at the Bult Inn and wrote a letter asking Henrietta and her new husband, Charles, to join them in Egmondse for the holidays. It was far easier for the new couple to travel from London to Egmondse than to Weimar.

Corinne adored being back in Egmondse as she looked out across the village of tiny fishing houses. She gulped in breaths of the fresh sea air. She pulled her scarf in tighter to her neck as she and Gari walked through the market.

"Let's set up a tree for the children like we did that first year I arrived here," Corinne said. Corinne searched until she found a rather tall tree.

"We'll have to put it up in the studio barn," Gari said.

"I'm going to call on Miggles and have her help us with it," Corinne said. Her cheeks blushed with the cold.

Gari, Corinne, and Henrietta spent hours decorating the tree. They thought they had enough candy and gifts on the tree for one hundred children. They tried to keep it a secret, but soon the word got out. The villagers had noticed that their resident painter had returned.

"I'm going to dress you up as Santa Claus," Corinne said.

"You mean Sinterklaas," Gari said. "The hardest part for me will be acting nice!"

"Maybe you should be dressed as Piet then," Corinne smiled. Her husband could be cold at times but never at Christmas.

Gari pulled on some red trousers and a red cloak. He finished his costume with a red hat. He chose not to wear the white bishop's garb underneath.

"Now all you need is a white horse!" Henrietta exclaimed.

In the end, the children focused on stuffing themselves with cakes and candy and pulling gifts from the tree, not so much on Gari dressed as Santa Claus.

Chapter 9

1910: The Birthday and Queen's Day

On February 27, 1910, Corinne celebrated her thirtieth birthday. She and Gari hosted a dinner party with their friends, Carl and Emma. Because the celebration was so soon after Valentine's Day, Corinne strung red paper hearts from the chandelier over the table to the four corners of the room. The highlight of the celebration was a fruitcake with candles on it, as was the custom in Germany. Corinne missed Miggles, who now lived in London. She tried to have the same kind of friendship with Emma that she had had with Henrietta, but the two ladies were so different.

For the party, Corinne wore a white turtleneck blouse with puffy, frilly sleeves and a vee-shaped front embroidered in gold thread. Gari looked dapper in a brown suit.

Although it was frosty outside, Gari gave her a cornucopia-shaped vase filled with her favorite cut winter roses. She thought she would paint the arrangement later in the week.

"Happy birthday, my darling," he said, and kissed her lightly on the lips.

"Thank you. The roses are beautiful," Corinne said as she lowered her face into the bouquet and inhaled deeply. "And they smell wonderful, too."

"Luckily, you weren't a leapling," Emma said, as they clinked their wine glasses together.

"A few more days and I would have been one," Corinne said. She set her wine glass down, formed her hands into a prayer in front of her chest, and looked up to the ceiling. "Thank you, Mother, for being expedient as usual."

"Maybe it's not such a bad thing to only have a birthday every four years," Emma said.

"She's already twenty-two years younger than me. We don't need any more gap than that!" Gari exclaimed. Everyone laughed.

"And she's not a leapling. She's my liebling," Gari said, endearingly. The corners of Gari's eyes crinkled slightly as he smiled at her.

"I read in the newspaper that President Roosevelt and his son Kermit are coming to Germany in May. The Kaiser is looking forward to their visit. Will they be visiting his portraiture artist?" Carl asked.

"Ex-president now. And I rather think not. They have been hunting in the Sudan from what I've read. Roosevelt killed one giant bull eland," Gari said.

"What exactly is an eland?" Emma asked.

"It's a type of large antelope. Faun-colored with black, twisted horns," Gari answered.

"Why do they have to kill those magnificent animals?" Corinne wondered aloud.

"It's a way for men to show off their high social status. Bragging rights," Carl said.

"I know I helped to dress him as a hunter for his portrait, but now I'm repulsed by it," Corinne said.

"Speaking of portraits and artwork, have you talked to the director of the Kunsthall about exhibiting your paintings?" Carl asked Corinne.

"Even with all the paintings I've done, I never feel quite ready for any exhibit, but I plan to speak with him this summer. As the exhibit is later in the summer, that should still give me enough time to pull some pieces together," Corinne replied.

They picked up their wine glasses from the table and moved to the parlor.

"Now that we're finished with dinner, let's play a game!" Corinne exclaimed. "Dogs and Cats! Before you got here, I had our maid hide an entire deck of cards in the dining room and parlor. Gari and I will be the Dogs. Gari will be our Captain. Emma and Carl, you will be the Cats. Carl, you will be the 'Captain of the Cats.'"

"How does one play this game?" Carl asked.

"Dogs will search the house for black cards. Cats will search for red. If I find a black card, I will stand and 'Woof!' loudly until Gari rushes over to me to fetch my card. If Emma finds a red card, she will stand and 'Meow!' loudly until you retrieve her card. Of course, if you or Gari find a card, there is no barking or meowing necessary," Corinne explained.

Corinne had already spied the corner of a black card under a lamp.

"Woof!" she said as she slid the card out and Gari hurried to her side.

"Oh, and I forgot to say, if you find an opposing team's card, you can hide it somewhere even harder to locate. And the first team to assemble their half of the deck is the winner!" Corinne said, her face flushed with excitement.

They scurried around the room, picking up lamps and vases. Emma found a couple of cards tucked inside of books on the bookshelf and she was meowing over and over. Carl hurtled the back of the sofa to get to her. Corinne laughed so hard that her stomach hurt.

"We won!" Carl shouted. "That was the last one. We have all of our cards!"

The von Schirachs bundled up in their warm winter coats, thanked the Melchers for the lovely evening, and went home. It had been a cheerful birthday party for Corinne.

*

For Queen's Day in 1910, Gari and Corinne made a brief return trip to Egmondse aan den Hoef. Corinne loved the Dutch coast much more than she cared for her home in Germany. The women in town strung clotheslines across the streets with orange shirts, towels, and handkerchiefs, creating a gay promenade to walk through. The whole of Holland seemed dressed in orange to celebrate. The spring weather fell in sync with the April holiday.

Corinne loved the street games that everyone played. Her favorite had to be spijkerpoepen. Men tied a piece of string around their waists and at the end of the string dangling behind their backs, they tied a nail. Someone set a beer bottle on the street and the men had to squat over the beer bottle to try to drop the nail into the bottle, as if they were pooping the nail into the bottle. Corinne thought it was hilarious.

"Do you want to join in?" Corinne asked Gari.

"Absolutely not!" Gari huffed. He steered his giggling wife away from the games and towards the flea market sales, set up in a quieter part of town.

As Gari and Corinne walked through the flea market, they stumbled upon a lovely portrait on a wooden panel for sale at one of the houses. It was a large painting, three feet wide by four feet tall with the title *Young Girl with a Fan* scrawled across the back. The little girl was dressed in a brown brocade gown with a stiff white lace collar, and she stood on a black and white checkerboard floor. In her right hand she held a fan of ostrich feathers.

"I feel like this is by an old Dutch Master from the 1600s." Gari scrutinized the painting. The frame leaned against the house; he pulled it out so that it stood vertically.

"Even if it isn't from one of the Masters, it's a lovely painting of a young girl. She appears to be on a stage," Corinne said.

"Or it could be a painting of a dwarf. It was common for court painters to include dwarfs in their paintings. She stands so stiff and rigid. The costume is outstanding," Gari said.

"Let's buy it. I adore it," Corinne said.

Gari took the painting home and hung it in the parlor, next to one of his father's sculpted wooden cuckoo clocks.

Corinne loved to stop and look at the painting whenever she passed it during her day. Intense and energetic, it made her feel happy. It was so different from Gari's interpretations of children. The painter's flow was palpable to her. She took great pleasure from the expression in the little girl's eyes. She wanted to talk to her, confide in her, and ask her if it was time to submit her own paintings to the Salon again. What would the little girl answer if she could?

When Corinne and Gari returned to Germany in May, they read in the newspaper that Halley's Comet was expected to be visible as the Earth was going to pass through the comet's tail. The article gave a brief history on the comet. The first representation of Halley's Comet in art had been on the Bayeaux Tapestry in Normandy. Its appearance had signaled the end of Anglo-Saxon rule.

"What are you thinking about?" Gari asked. He noticed Corinne biting her bottom lip as they sat in the parlor one evening after dinner. Corinne was working on her embroidery and Gari was sipping a glass of port.

"I can't take my mind off what you read in the newspaper this morning about the comet. I've been seeing so many signs in things lately. Do you really think the comet is a bad omen, as everyone's been saying?" Corinne asked.

"A French astronomer, Camille Flammarion, says that a poisonous gas in its tail may snuff out all life on the planet. The near approach of it never fails to stir up some rumpus. But I don't think we should worry about it too much. Didn't you just go to an astrologist and have your tarot cards read? And didn't she say that you shouldn't worry?" Gari asked. Corinne had recently become curious about tarot decks. She loved the bright colors of the artwork on the cards.

"I know that worrying doesn't really help. And that's what I meant about the signs, lately. The astrologist told me there would be opportunities for me and a period of clarity after a time of confusion. She said I should follow my heart and live my passion. Do you think the comet is a sign that there will be more brightness and fullness in my life?" Corinne asked.

"I believe that you are the strongest, smartest person I know. Never forget that. You don't need a comet to give you a sign. You can do anything you set your mind to," Gari answered.

"Let's go outside and see if we can find the tail in the sky," Corinne said. She was somewhat stunned by what her husband had just shared. As darkness approached, they walked outside of the house and through the park to a quiet spot by the River Ilm. They walked past the five-meter-high chunk of travertine called the Dessau Stone. They sat on a bench close to the riverbank and held hands. The woods were quiet and the sound of rustling water flowing in the river relaxed them. Corinne leaned against Gari's warm body.

"We really are blessed to do work that we both love. It gives fullness to our lives. You know that any time I look at something, I'm painting it in my mind," Corinne said, and snuggled closer to her husband.

"Wouldn't it be great to do a painting of the sky with the comet shooting by?" Gari gazed into the night sky.

"I think you should put a comet in one of your paintings, but don't tell anyone about it. See if anyone figures it out. I have a few other ideas for my next painting, not related to the comet," she said. They never saw the comet's tail that night and they returned to their house.

Corrine decided to do a painting of the parlor in her German house and include the *Young Girl with a Fan* in her painting. She wanted to show the depth of her craft by painting the young girl in the style of Dutch masters like Rubens and van Dyke; and then finish the painting in her own style. She showed the illusion of space in the parlor. The walls, up to the wainscoting in the parlor, were painted pink; green and pink flowers were stenciled in a small strip directly above the wainscoting. Corinne also included a vase of flowers on the table in front of the painting, staying true to her still life roots. She had studied the shadows and how the light reflected. Fittingly, she called the painting *The Pink Room.*

Corinne felt a sense of joy and calm with this painting, and that she was on a journey with her artwork. In some ways, this painting felt like a birthing to her. It was a difficult painting technically, but it had come from her so easily. She wanted this painting to be out in the world and planned to enter it in the German art show, Neue Kunst der Moderne.

At the beginning of summer, Corinne packed up three of her paintings to ship to the Kunsthall. These were the works she thought best represented her artistic vision. She included the introductory letter from Carl. She was over the moon when she got the reply in the mail that all three pieces would be exhibited. She was so proud to finally have her paintings on a wall in a museum. This was the validation she had been seeking since the Salon. Perhaps the comet was a sign after all.

On the other hand, Corinne was also terrified to go and see her artwork up on the walls. Essentially stating that "my art deserves to be exhibited" was so bold that it frightened her.

Gari and Corinne made the trip to Mannheim and approached the towering fortress of the Art Nouveau building. Gari held her hand as they walked up the stairs, wedged between two daunting lions. She wondered if he could feel her trembling hand through her glove.

"I feel like I'm floating," Corinne said. Her mouth was so dry she could hardly swallow.

"You will see that it's like getting patted on the back and handed a free ice cream," Gari said.

"I could use that ice cream right now," she said.

When they entered the gallery, she immediately went to where her first piece was hanging. *The Pink Room* stood out next to two other paintings of interior spaces.

"I'm so pleased with the movement and use of vibrant colors in that piece," Corinne said. Gari agreed.

"I created a beautiful painting, whether it was exhibited or not," Corinne said.

"That is what I've been trying to tell you," Gari said.

Chapter 10

1914: The Great War

On August 1, 1914, Germany declared war on Russia. But instead of attacking Russia, on August 3, Germany moved first against France by sending its major armies through Belgium to capture Paris from the north.

Gari continued to paint scenes featuring his home in North Holland. *The Crimson Rambler* was a painting of the rose arbor in his garden; a tree and lawn statue stood in the background. His broken brushwork and use of light pastel colors in this painting made it more impressionistic than any of his previous works. Corinne, missing her old garden near the dunes, would gaze at the painting and imagine herself walking down the garden path.

Corinne had loved tending the rose garden, planting strawberries, and caring for fruit trees in her back garden. Luek had died a few years before, and Corinne made a section of their garden into a pet cemetery. She placed a small headstone and a statue of a dog to mark the site where his remains were buried. The headstone read, "He was only a dog, but he was human enough to be great comfort in hours of loneliness."

The dogs Corinne saw in Germany were working dogs. In town, she saw a weathered wooden cart with a dog harnessed to the shaft on one side, while an old, stooped woman gripped the shaft on the other side, sharing the burden of pulling the load. On Mondays, the carts were filled with laundry baskets. Wherever there was water flowing, there were little stands erected for laundry work. The women all kneeled, using a stone, or board, for rubbing and soaping the clothes against the current. *Women certainly work hard here*, Corinne thought.

Everyone in town believed the war would be quick and decisive. Flags flew on all of the houses as if they were decorated for a festival. In the courtyard, a band gave a concert every day at noon and a contingent of soldiers goosestepped around the square. Corinne sent her maid to the market to buy food and staples as the locals flocked to the city centers to show their support for the war. Corinne thought her grandparents must have felt the same way at the start of the Civil War. They would be heroes defending their homeland. Her Grandfather Lawton had been a Brigadier General and then served as the Quartermaster General for the Confederate States Army.

As the months wore on, food became more and more scarce. She told their maid to store potatoes in the cellar. The "rice" lamb chop became a weekly dinner: The meal was composed of rice boiled and molded into a lump that resembled a lamp chop, and a wooden skewer was jabbed into the lump to resemble the bone. A little paper rosette attached to the bone made the illusion complete. The Melchers' maid fried the chops in mutton talon and when she brought it to the table, it smelled like the real thing. She also made a vegetable beefsteak with cornmeal, spinach, potatoes, ground nuts, and an egg to bind it together. It looked like beef until Gari cut into the center with his knife to reveal the green interior. In September, Corinne gasped as she read in the paper that the elephants in the Berlin Zoo had been butchered for their meat.

In October, German bakers were permitted to make bread using potato flour. This resulted in K-Brot or Kartoffeln Brot *potato bread,* also known as Krieg Brot *war bread.* Ersatz, meaning replacement, became a common term. Continuing shortages led to rationing.

Many of the teachers and students at the school went off to fight in the war, but Gari stayed and kept the school operating for the remaining students. As he wasn't a German national, he wasn't required to fight. His role as an art educator was important to the German government for maintaining cultural continuity.

It wasn't long before the first death lists were published in the newspaper. It was a great shock to see that most of the officers were dead within the first few weeks, along with many young soldiers. The passion for the war faded quickly.

Corinne wanted to continue with her painting and produce as she had been doing for the last ten years, but she also felt like she needed a break. The very idea of painting felt like a fifty-pound weight on her chest when so much was going on in the world. She felt a little lost and confused. As much as she wanted to submit work to the Salon again, the war brought a closure to that idea. The Salon was continuing throughout the years of war but in a modified capacity. Much of the work depicted war scenes or reflected the hardship of the times. Now that Germany was at war, she wasn't sure if the Kunsthall would have another show where she could exhibit.

Besides her painting, Corrine was accomplished at embroidery. Women embroidered household items to sell in America, and she felt she would be more of a help to the United States with her sewing. She thought if she did something like this, she would still feel creative. She began embroidering images onto dish towels of soldiers, flags, coats of arms, even Paris with planes flying overhead, and she sent them to her friends and family back in Baltimore and Savannah. Even though her life wasn't going as she had planned, Corinne found some goodness.

The post didn't always go through, but she continued to write to her friend Henrietta in London. Sometimes she received letters in return. Gari and Corinne had received word in August of the previous year that their old friend George Hitchcock died from heart failure. He had been living on a houseboat moored at the Island of Marken in Holland. They hadn't seen him in years.

> Dear Miggles,
>
> How are you managing in London with the war going on? It is difficult to obtain food here sometimes. Is that true there? I suppose you always have the fruits of the sea.
>
> So far, the Germans in town have been very respectful of us. The men tip their hats to me when I walk past them. There have been plenty of airplanes overhead. But on a quiet day with birds singing outside, one wonders if there is a war on. I continue to feel so anxious.
>
> Remember me to the children.
>
> Your loving friend,
> Corinne

> Dear Corinne,
>
> It was great to get your letter. I think of you often, stuck in the middle of Weimar, Germany. I hear from my children that

the Netherlands is remaining neutral during the war, but they watch for the U-boots and mines in the harbor. And there are a few refugees from Belgium. They have some trouble getting food due to the blockades. They tell me that the women in town continue to mend their fishing nets and life goes on.

Also, I'm not sure if you've been told, but the Albright Art Gallery in Buffalo, New York held a luncheon in honor of George. His wife Cecil was the guest of honor. They are showing a retrospective of George's flower field paintings.

I miss our warm conversations, my dear friend.

My love to you and Gari,

Miggles

Corinne knew Gari grieved for his friend, but he was private in his grief. She caught him sitting in his studio sometimes with tears in his eyes. He didn't share those feelings with her and quickly wiped his face when he heard her enter.

*

In September, Gari and Corinne retreated to Holland. Gari wanted to put some finishing touches on some new paintings, and he found it difficult to concentrate in Germany. Gari stopped at a shop to pick up some food before they ventured back to their home and studio on the dunes.

"The whole of Europe is ablaze and at war. Was there ever anything like it?" Gari asked the shopkeeper.

"Terrible. Simply inconceivable," the shopkeeper answered.

"I can think of nothing but the horror of it, and this thought of wholesale destruction and agony makes me sick and sad," Gari said. Corinne thought he could never say such things at the school in Weimar. Those statements would be considered treasonous. The German government enforced strict laws against hostile speech or anti-patriotic gossip.

"Even here in neutral Holland, one's mind is absorbed and one's heart so sore at the thought of this calamity," the shopkeeper said.

"Can Holland continue neutral? We are perhaps only in the beginning of this fearful struggle," Gari said.

"Lord knows how it will end," the shopkeeper said.

As autumn turned to winter, the new thought was that the war would be over by Christmas, so Gari and Corinne returned to Weimar. At the beginning of December, the town celebrated St. Barbara's day.

The townspeople set up a Christmas market. An older man in a Santa costume appeared in the village center wearing a papier mâché mask with a wispy white cotton beard. He donned a red cloth cap, coat, pants with a strapping black belt, and a gift bag that matched his fleece coat. He gingerly sat on an imitation brick chimney, made from a wooden box. Children lined up to tell him what they wanted for gifts. Afterwards, they sang Christmas carols.

Corinne set up a small tree in their parlor next to the fireplace. She put lighted candles in the windows. On Christmas Eve, the couple hung tinsel and lit candles on its branches. The tree filled the house with a pine scent, but it didn't fill her heart with joy as the trees had done in the past in Egmondse. She played "Silent Night" and "Away in a Manger" on the piano for Gari to help them into the Christmas spirit. Several inches of snow fell, but it quickly turned to slush. As much as they tried to celebrate, they couldn't forget about the war.

Corinne drew a small, handmade calendar for Gari's gift. On the top of each month's page, she made a drawing of something from their past year together.

"What a wonderful gift," Gari said. "I shall keep it in my studio and write all my appointments in it."

Gari pulled Corinne onto his lap as they sat next to their beautiful tree and the crackling fireplace. He gave her a small velvet box. She opened it to reveal a stunning gold necklace.

"It's beautiful!" she said.

"We're going to get through this war. Let's remember that," Gari said.

On New Year's Eve, Gari and Corinne conjured their American spirit with tin horns and confetti. As Gari lifted his glass for a toast, he said somberly, "Let's have a toast to the dead in the present war." They clinked glasses together. "Obviously, the war was not over by Christmas as the government predicted," Gari continued. Although he was holding up his champagne flute, his shoulders drooped.

"Both sides thought it would be a brief war with all their new weapons. But just like the Civil War, a quick victory did not come," Corinne said.

"Machine guns, tanks, chemical gas, airplanes… such horrible weapons." Gari bowed his head as he spoke.

"Let's hope it's over soon," Corinne added as she gazed at the lights on her Christmas tree. Despite the dreariness of the previous years, they both sought to greet the new year with enthusiasm and confidence.

Chapter 11

1915: The Pan-American Exposition

On May 7, 1915, German U-boats sank the British ocean liner, Lusitania, with over one hundred Americans on board. As tensions grew due to the increased submarine warfare, Corinne and Gari decided to leave Germany to return to the United States.

"I'm very nervous about traveling across the ocean now, with U-boats everywhere," Corinne said.

"We'll be okay, my dear. It takes only six days. We will treat it just like the ocean voyage where we met, so many years ago," Gari said.

Gari packed all his paintings in crates to carry along with them, and the couple traveled by train, first to Amsterdam, and then by a small steam ship to Liverpool to board a large English steamer bound for New York. They chose the ship because it had a military escort. Gari obtained insurance and documented all his paintings before the trip. Corinne had one day to see her friends before their ship departed.

The ship had been painted a war gray and was illuminated by very few lights. At sea, the portholes in all of the cabins were covered with black paper. There were few passengers on the ship but there was a mix of elite travelers, business travelers and immigrants. Gari and Corinne played cards in their cabin to pass the time. They did venture into the library to sit at the rosewood writing tables with chairs upholstered in rose-colored velvet. The luxury made them feel as though they were not even sailing.

"I wish we had taken a Scandinavian ship. They travel under neutral flags," Corinne said when they ventured out onto the deck in the early evening. The only light came from the moon.

"The moonlight is reflected in your eyes. You are bewitching," Gari said as he continued to try to keep Corinne's mind off the chance that there may be German submarines nearby. He put his arm around her as they leaned against the railing and looked out across the sea.

They dined with a mother and daughter who were traveling to the States to collect supplies for the British Red Cross in France, Mrs. Baron Fry and her daughter, Marianne. Dinner was a simple beef stew with bread but was served in the opulent dining room with mahogany paneled walls.

"As the number of injured soldiers increases, we must look for more ways to care for them. We have several convalescent centers, but it never seems to be enough. And we set up recreation rooms to keep up morale," Mrs. Fry said.

"We're also hoping to raise some money to purchase a couple of ambulances," Marianne said. "It's important to get the wounded and sick men away from the fighting."

"It's important work," Corinne said. "I commend your strength and spirit."

"Thank you, dear," Mrs. Fry said.

Corinne lived only for the moment when she would walk down the gangplank and step onto American soil. She stood at the ship's deck railing as they passed the Statue of Liberty.

The pink granite colonnade of the Chelsea Piers was a welcome site for Corinne despite having to wade through all the other passengers in the warehouse-like structure. Along the length of the pier were large metal signs marked with initials, marking where the passengers' luggage was waiting. They collected their items at the "M", got through customs, and headed to their apartment, just above Gari's studio in midtown at 80 West 40th Street.

Gari painted New York scenes from the windows, at Bryant Park, and of boats on the Hudson River. As much as she had loved the serenity of the Dutch coast, Corinne also loved the hustle and bustle of New York City.

On the morning of the Fourth of July, they both got up early and walked in the slight drizzle to Central Park. Mrs. C. L. Morehouse, the widow of Dr. Morehouse, whose father had fought with George Washington, read the Declaration of Independence when the American flag was raised at the Block House.

Promptly at noon, they heard a salute of forty-eight guns at Governor's Island.

On their way back to the apartment, Gari and Corinne walked through Times Square. When an occasional firecracker went off, Corinne jumped. On one building, the largest American flag ever made, at 165 feet long, was unfurled. The New York Fire Department band played "The Star-Spangled Banner" as the flag shimmered through the raindrops. Corinne felt a catch in her throat at the sight of it.

Dressed in white with a red, white, and blue sash, Corinne sauntered down the avenue. Gari was dashing in a linen suit with a straw hat. Both she and Gari walked with their umbrellas aloft amid a throng of umbrellas. They stopped at a street-side stand for a hot dog and a lemonade.

Before they left Times Square, the couple paused between bites of hot dog to listen to a speech about America's president keeping the United States out of the war in Europe. The sea of people then sang "Dixie," and "Yankee Doodle." A car decorated with red, white, and blue electric lights drove up to the bandstand where the speaker stood. A man and woman, dressed as Uncle Sam and Columbia, jumped from the car and danced. The crowd roared with applause.

All the festivities exhausted them, and when Gari and Corinne got back to their apartment, they went to bed and immediately fell asleep.

*

"At the end of July, we'll be leaving for San Francisco, Peachy," Gari said to Corinne over breakfast the next morning. "We'll meet John Sargent there and set up my exhibition room in the Pan-American Exposition. There is a great Palace of Fine Art, and I will be able to display several dozen of my paintings." This would be the couple's first visit out west.

"I wonder if it will be any cooler in the West than it is here. New York is stifling in the summer," Corinne said. She wiped the perspiration from her face and neck with a cool, damp handkerchief as she heard the children splashing in the fountain at Bryant Park.

"Do you remember that enormous flag in Times Square yesterday?"

"How could I forget it? It brought tears to my eyes," Corinne said.

"That will be displayed at the Pan-American Exposition. I just read that in the newspaper," Gari said.

Gari and Corinne stopped in Detroit on their way to San Francisco to spend a few days at Gari's boyhood home on Seyburn Avenue. In Gari's hometown, he was known to be the greatest living realist painter. During their stay, he granted an interview to a local newspaper.

When asked by the reporter about the expo, "The Cubists, Futurists, and their ilk will have little space and arouse little interest. They, and the furor their efforts created several years ago, are all but forgotten," Gari said.

"What do you mean by that?" the reporter asked.

"Picasso, Braque, and Magritte are part of a fad," Gari smugly replied. Corinne wished he would not be so boastful, but she couldn't stop him. She knew he didn't fully appreciate the growing influence of these artists.

They continued to San Francisco.

When they arrived at the site of the fair, Corinne couldn't stop staring at the Tower of Jewels. It was over five hundred feet tall and covered with cut-glass gems. They walked down the street of the Harbor View area to the Palace of Fine Arts, an open rotunda that bordered a lagoon. In a small, dark green side room behind the rotunda that housed the artist's exhibits, they ran into John Sargent. The walls in his room were covered with white cheesecloth, but the green still shone through.

"John, good to see you! What is going on here?" Gari asked as he shook hands with his stocky friend. Corinne stood behind him.

"I'm rehanging some of my paintings. Some of my friends tried to hang them the way I requested but I'm not happy with the result," John said. He smoked one cigarette after another.

"I rather like the cheesecloth canopy," Corinne said.

"I don't know. I think it covers some of the light, making it difficult to see my paintings," he said, as he nervously picked at an edge of the canopy.

Central to the exhibit was his portrait of author Henry James.

"This is the first time I'm showing this portrait in the United States. And you know I had decided never to do another portrait again, but here it is," John continued.

"Isn't this the same portrait that was damaged by a suffragette's ax when it was exhibited at the Royal Academy in London?" Corinne asked.

"This is the one," John said. John pointed to a few carefully restored cuts on the subject's face.

"The time for women is now, to unleash our gifts and do our creative work," Corinne said. "It's time for women to change the world. I wish she hadn't damaged your painting, but I think that's what she was trying to say."

"It really was just bad timing. Had nothing to do with Henry James himself. She just wanted to show that until women got the political rights they deserve, we should not feel that our art treasures are secure," he said.

"I suppose if a woman had painted it, she wouldn't have attacked it, because a woman's painting wouldn't have been worth as much," Corinne said, almost to herself, as John was busy moving smaller paintings from place to place. Corinne hadn't marched with the Suffragettes, but she believed in their cause.

To the right of the portrait of Henry James was a life-size nude of an Italian girl, an earlier piece. Beside that was a portrait of Secretary of State John Hay, arguably not one of Sargent's best works. On the opposite wall was an 1884 canvas of the French beauty, Mme. Gautreau. However, his portrait bust, *Rose,* was his best work; the bust's white scarf showed his masterful technique in painting the brocade texture. Several of his courtyard and stable scenes were peppered throughout.

"As you can see, Gari, they have hung the paintings willy-nilly. I'm trying to make sense of them. You should go and see how your room is laid out," John said.

Gari and Corinne entered the room next to Sargent's. Twenty-one oil paintings that had traveled with them on the ship from Weimar. His superbly painted *The Fencing Master* greeted fair goers with his foil extended as they stepped into the room. Opposite this was a painting of a young mother bent over her nursing baby. There were several of his paintings from his Dutch period. *The Skaters* showed a young Dutch couple carrying their ice skates. There was another of a young Dutch mother nursing her baby, dressed in full costume, while another child rests at her knee. The colors of her outfit popped in front of the green meadow background. The theme of the mother and child continued in Gari's painting titled *Smithy.*

"This is the painting that James Deering loaned to the exhibit," Gari said. It was another young mother and small child painting where both figures gazed at you with a look of wonder. It was a very pleasant picture despite having been painted in browns and grays.

The most dominating painting in the room was a portrait of art collector, Hugo Reisinger. He sits in front of a canvas while Gari stands behind him clad in shirtsleeves and a yellow waistcoat with a palette and brushes in his hand.

"You didn't do yourself justice in this painting, Mr. M," Corinne said. "Although the fact that you're holding a palette and brushes is always accurate."

Corinne had started calling Gari by the nickname "Mr. M" years before when he began affectionately calling her "Peachy." Down south, the custom of using Mr. with the first initial of the last name as a nickname was considered a sign of respect and endearment.

Interspersed throughout these paintings were a few sunny interiors of women sewing or reading, or maids at work.

"What do you think of the general layout, Corinne?" Gari asked.

"I think it works. And I'm happy they kept the walls painted white, so the paintings stand out—unlike in John's dark room," she said. "I think the fencer is guarding the women in the room. And as the viewer, you're at the back of it all, taking it all in."

When Christmas came around again, Corinne thought about her friend Emma, still in Germany. She prepared a package of cookies with nuts in them, some canned pickled vegetables and preserves, a little chocolate for the children, and heavy woolen socks for the whole family.

Corinne didn't want to focus entirely on the war overseas. She completed a personalized journal as a gift for Gari. In all the places they had lived and visited, Egmondse aan Zee, Paris, San Francisco, and New York City, she had sketched images of interesting letters or fonts. For Christmas, she wanted to put together some of the letters along with descriptions of Gari's personality. She had sketched the vertical sign on the Knickerbocker Hotel in Times Square. She was going to use the "K" to describe how kind she thought Gari was.

Gari was delighted with the gift. In response, he began doing the same thing and sketched images of letters and signs that he found interesting. It became a game between them. They would include miniature illustrations of letters and decorative borders when they sent messages to one another, in the style of illuminated manuscripts. In the spirit of fun, Gari and Corinne began competing to create more elaborate and striking sketches than the other.

Chapter 12

1916: Belmont

Gari and Corinne loved their apartment and studio in New York City, but they yearned for a quieter life after all the tension of the war in Europe. After searching for a property that was close to the rail lines to Washington DC and New York City, they found and purchased a country estate in Falmouth, Virginia. The eighteenth century, two-story, white frame, Georgian house was perched on a ridge above the Rappahannock River. The property was in bad condition when they purchased it, but they enjoyed financial security, so renovation was not an issue. The property included a small kitchen cottage and a dairy. Once the renovations were complete, they decorated their home with artwork they had collected during their travels. An unexpected perk of the property was that the Falmouth bridge was part of the sale, and they collected tolls on the bridge to pay for its upkeep. They called their new estate Belmont, the name derived from the French words, "belle" and "mont" for "beautiful mountain." Corinne was happy to be settled in one place.

She wanted to get another dog. In San Francisco, John Sargent had told her the story of the "illusive greyhound." The Minturn family had commissioned him to paint a wedding portrait of Newton Phelps Stokes and Edith Minturn in New York City. He wanted to paint Mrs. Stokes standing in informal walking attire with a large dog beside her. A portrait by Dutch artist, Anthony van Dyke, of James Stuart at the Metropolitan Museum of Art inspired him. In this painting, Stuart's right hand strokes the head of a magnificent greyhound; the dog loyally leans against his owner's side.

Unfortunately, John couldn't find a suitable dog, and Mr. Stokes good-naturedly let his wife take center stage. John finally painted Mrs. Stokes in the same stance as Stuart in the van Dyke painting, replacing the dog with a straw boater's hat. She became the subject of the painting; Mr. Stokes stands in the background, in the shadow of his wife. The painting played homage to the idea of the "New Woman." And the painting and its story was one of the reasons Corinne wanted to have a greyhound as a pet.

"Many of the Dutch and Flemish masters painted portraits of men with hound-type dogs by their sides. The dog would emulate the owner's emotions. It was a status symbol," Gari said to Corinne.

"And why are most women painted with little lap dogs?" Corinne asked.

"Maybe their dresses make it too difficult to pose the dog close enough to them for a painting," Gari offered.

"Well, I'm going to get a greyhound now that we've bought this wonderful property in Virginia. Mother knows someone in the Maryland Kennel Club, and they'll recommend a puppy for me. And you can figure out how to position both of us in a painting," Corinne said.

In the spring, the brindle greyhound arrived at Belmont. The couple named her Ivy. Corinne sewed beautiful, jeweled collars for her to wear. Ivy was constantly at Corinne's side.

Keeping up with the extensive property proved too much for the Melchers alone. Gari's hair had turned gray as he approached his 56th birthday. He had crow's feet around his eyes. Although he was still broad and burly, painting was enough of a task for him. He would leave work on the house and grounds to a younger man.

"There is a local man here named Mason Dillon, and I'd like to hire him as a groundman," Gari said.

"I will continue to take care of my roses. It won't be necessary for Mr. Dillon to attend to them. And I'd like you to hire a local woman, Sarah Lucas, as a housekeeper. She comes highly recommended." Corinne said.

The Dillons moved into the cook's house that was on the property. Sarah took a room next to the kitchen in the main house. In the room was a small cot and a basin for washing up. Corinne showed Sarah around the house and explained her duties to her.

"Sarah, we would like you to work from seven until five every day except for Sundays. You may have Sunday to do as you wish, but we would like you to cook some things ahead of time and leave them in the icebox for us. Cook three meals a day for us when we are at the house, and I will expect that you cook extra special foods when we have guests," Corinne said.

"Yes, ma'am," Sarah said as she followed along behind her mistress. Corinne demonstrated to Sarah where items were stored by opening and closing cabinets in the kitchen.

"We would also like you to keep the house clean and help me take care of my animals. My birds and dogs are very important to me. Of course, we get eggs from the chickens, and we can use their feathers for bedding. It makes the estate more self-sufficient," Corinne said.

"Yes, ma'am," Sarah nodded. "I love animals, so that won't be a problem for me." Sarah hesitated, "Ma'am?"

"Yes?"

"What would you like me to call you?"

"Mrs. Melchers will be fine," Corinne said.

"Yes, ma'am. Mrs. Melchers," Sarah said.

Upon settling in her Belmont house, Corinne volunteered to host a lawn party to raise funds for the Red Cross War Fund. Women at the party sat at tables and put together packages of writing supplies, socks, sewing kits, playing cards, and chewing gum to send to the soldiers overseas. Sarah wore a white apron over her black skirt and served lemonade to the women as they worked.

Beforehand, Corinne had filled the yard around Belmont with chickens, turkeys, and ducks. Even a few peacocks wandered among party tables making squawking sounds like crying babies. Ivy, never far from Corinne's side, behaved well, not chasing the birds. The ladies at the lawn party enjoyed seeing the birds preen around their tables.

"I understand that Mrs. Melchers is the niece of the Confederate Military Officer, General E. P. Alexander," whispered Mrs. Willis, the wife of the President of the Farmers and Merchants Bank. Sitting beside her was Mrs. Baldwin, the owner of the neighboring estate, Snowden, in Bowling Green.

"I intend to welcome her with open arms. Why don't we have a Sunday lunch at Snowden within the next few weeks," Mrs. Baldwin said, behind her fan.

Corinne overheard the conversation as she neared their table. She walked up onto her porch to address the women. A few ladies began tapping their water glasses with their knives so that the chatter would stop, and they could hear what Corinne had to say.

"Good afternoon, ladies. I'm so pleased that you could join us for my first lawn party at Belmont. Now that the United States has entered the war, I know that many of us have friends and family in Europe. My grandfather, Alexander Lawton, was a Brigadier General and the Quarter Master General of the Confederate States Army. He was seriously wounded at the Battle of Antietam. After the war, he served as the Ambassador to the Austrian court of Franz Joseph the First. I believe we were all touched by the War Between the States. After all the threatening war clouds here and seeing first-hand what is going on in Europe, I'm happy we can play this small part to help the American Red Cross."

The group applauded and Corinne smiled to herself, thinking that she had corrected Mrs. Willis' mix-up of her grandfather with her uncle, without having to call her out on it directly.

After the success of the lawn party, Corinne became a patroness for the Red Cross entertainment at the Opera House in Fredericksburg, a beautiful brick building at the corner of William and Caroline Streets. Before the opera began, Corinne invited the entire student population of the Normal School, an all-girls school, to come onto the stage. Dressed in white, they marched three abreast across the stage. The women on the right donned red sashes while those on the left wore blue ones; the group in the middle divided the two colors with white sashes. Each carried an American flag, and some carried banners telling of the war work their school had done. One banner proclaimed they had bought War Savings and Thrift Stamps, another that they had adopted a French war orphan, and another indicated how many sweaters they had knit for the soldiers. Corinne remembered the dinner on the ship with the Frys, and she wanted to do her part to help. She was pleased to send a check for $431.00 to the Red Cross when the event was over.

*

As Corinne had been used to rationing her food while in Germany, she continued to do so in Virginia. They ate locally procured game and fish whenever they could. She wrote a letter to the editor of the local paper telling him of ways a family could conserve their food supply. She encouraged students at the local schools to collect scrap metal and to roll bandages.

One evening, Gari and Corinne were having a dinner of curried venison and rice with a side of boiled rutabagas in their cheery dining room when Corinne blurted out, "I'm so worried about my brother Leonard. He's written me a letter that he wants to become an interpreter for the war."

Gari put down his knife and fork and took her hand in his. "Everyone must do what they feel is right," Gari said calmly. "If he is called to serve, he will be an officer. He won't be in the trenches. So, you mustn't worry."

Corinne was not convinced.

Leonard was the editor of the weekly satirical magazine, *Judge*. He had attended Plattsburgh Training Camp at Saranac Lake, New York, over the summer. The training camp came to be called "The Businessman's Camp" as the men who attended were all college-educated and on the path to becoming officers.

Corinne chewed on the inside of her lip and turned slowly to face her husband.

"Verdun is well fortified, and the Americans and the French are holding the Germans back," Gari said, adding to what he read in the newspapers every day.

"I know he would be supporting personnel. I hope you're correct about them holding the Germans back, but I'm not happy about it," Corinne said.

"He's your brother, so of course you feel that way about him," Gari said.

"I will respect his decision, but I don't have to like it," Corinne said.

"Why don't you write a return letter to him? Try to be supportive. I think it would be meaningful to him," Gari said.

Corinne nodded in agreement and returned to her meal.

"You know what we've completely forgotten? Tonight, is Halloween! Why don't we go into town tonight? I'll have Mr. Dillon hook up the carriage. It will take your mind off Leonard," Gari said.

Gari offered his hand to Corinne as she climbed up into the carriage. He covered their laps with a blanket to ward off the chill October air. Mr. Dillon made a clicking noise by hitting his tongue on the roof of his mouth and the horses moved forward down the gravel driveway.

Soon they were in town clip-clopping down Caroline Street with a crescent moon shining down on them. Houses and storefronts were decorated with cornstalks and jack o'lanterns made from squash and pumpkins. A bonfire burned somewhere nearby. On one side of the street, they saw a group of children, one dressed as a witch, another as a ghost, and another as a devil. Corinne smiled at the sight of them. They stopped at a crosswalk to let another group of children pass in front of them.

"Oh Gari. Look!" Corinne pointed. There was a little girl dressed in a Dutch girl costume, complete with wooden shoes.

"That costume is so sweet!"

"She's adorable," Gari agreed.

"What kind of costume would you wear, if you were still a child?" Corinne asked.

"I suppose some kind of a pirate or gypsy," Gari said. "And you?"

"I would be a crepe paper rose with a pink skirt with an abundance of netting underneath, and a green hat!"

"That does sound like you, my dear. And all handmade. I can picture it," Gari said.

Gari signaled for Mr. Dillon to turn the horses for home. Corinne snuggled close to Gari as they crossed the Rappahannock River back to Belmont.

Gari continued to travel back and forth to New York City on the train. He had a one-man show at the Montross Gallery, which was committed to representing American artists. Gari needed this exposure after having lived in Europe for so long. The impressive gallery, at 550 Fifth Avenue, held exhibitions with an admission cost of ten to twenty-five cents and sometimes as many as eight-hundred people went through to look at the artwork. This exhibition showed his versatility as a colorist. Corinne had modeled for one of his paintings in the show, *Women,* which displayed the interior of their New York apartment. In the painting, a woman stands in her bedroom having her colorful dress hemmed by a maid. The maid kneels next to the woman, dressed in black with a white apron and bonnet. Several paintings are on the walls and knick-knacks sit on the mantle of the fireplace. A striped chair and desk next to the window complete the tableau.

Gari's paintings showing domestic life were a small comfort to the public at large as the war continued to drag on in Europe. Corinne continued with her Red Cross duties, and any spare time she had for painting was all but nonexistent.

Chapter 13

1918: The Spanish Flu

In the spring of 1918, Corinne and Gari read stories in the newspapers about the influenza in the army camps. By May, it seemed that the influenza, soon to be known as the Spanish flu, was sweeping across the population. Forty percent of the country was afflicted with an influenza that quickly turned to pneumonia and even presented as sudden fits in some patients. The disease was highly contagious and developed rapidly. Soon the couple were reading reports of an epidemic of the disease in many cities in the world and people were dying in record numbers.

Nonetheless, Gari Melchers continued to create art. While hospitalized due to a severe stroke, Austrian artist Gustav Klimt contracted the flu. Less than a month later, he died. This news did not deter Gari from traveling to New York City by train from Belmont. At the height of the pandemic, Gari wrote from New York City as he organized his paintings for an exhibit at the Art Institute of Chicago.

> My dear Peachy,
>
> How are you? I hope the influenza is not getting worse in Falmouth and Fredericksburg. The influenza is very bad in this town. From your letter saying that the disease is raging I'm concerned about you. Here it exists badly enough but considering the size of New York, it is still comparatively small. But of course, it may get worse very soon.
>
> Let us hope for the best.
>
> I kiss you with all my heart and love,
>
> Mr. M

Gari minimized the severity of the disease outbreak in New York City. City officials implemented quarantine measures and setup temporary medical facilities. All schools, moving picture houses, theatres, and churches closed. Health officials persuaded New Yorkers to cover their mouths when they coughed or sneezed and asked them to stop spitting.

"We need nurses or any sensible women that know how to nurse the sick. We need them very badly," the health commissioner pled in a newspaper article.

The Art Institute of Chicago showed several collections of paintings that had bearing on the war. Pictures by the soldier artists of France and drawings by French schoolchildren. The collection of paintings that Gari referred to in his letter was for a show he was doing with Robert Henri titled, *Friends of Our Native Landscape.* Henri lived in New York and was known as a painter of urban landscapes. Gari had felt compelled to join him in the city to finalize their plans for the show, though Corinne failed to see the urgency, as gathering in large groups was prohibited. She wanted Gari to come home. Whenever she thought about the current situation, her chest tightened, and she found herself clenching her fists.

Corinne funneled her frustration into something she thought was useful. She made gauze masks for herself, her maid Sarah, and Sarah's son, Archie. She sent one to Gari in New York. The masks had three to four layers of rectangular gauze to cover the nose and mouth with a band around the back of the head. But Gari continued to be cavalier about the disease and entertained clients in his studio. Corinne didn't know if he wore the mask or not.

Corinne read in the local newspaper that the disease started with a chill or chills. Severe headache with pain in the legs, neck, and spine were present. Then came the "tired feeling" and soon after, feeling wretched all over. Fever blisters broke out on the sufferer's lips. The face became flushed with a fever between 102 and 104 degrees. A harsh cough sprayed airborne particles. Within four days the worst was usually over, or pneumonia set in.

Corinne was furious and frustrated with Gari for being so dismissive of the disease. He was older and at a higher risk of dying. His physical vulnerability made her feel vulnerable. She needed Gari. She sent him a letter in response to the one he had sent to her.

Dear Mr. M,

I need you. The way you are acting during this pandemic makes me feel as though you don't care about me. I feel all alone. Faced with this virus, we're all weak and at its mercy. Sarah, her son, and I have been locked in at Belmont. Ours is a beautiful home, but it is making me crazy.

Please come home,

Peachy

She became even more distraught when she received no reply from him. She turned to Sarah to help get herself through each day. Corinne would wander into the kitchen and cook and bake with Sarah to pass the time. Sarah showed Corinne how to cook cornmeal griddlecakes and blueberry muffins.

"If we skip a spoon of sugar, we'll help a soldier to go the extra mile in the war," Corinne said.

"We can skip the sugar altogether, Mrs. Melchers. I use molasses, corn syrup, and honey in my recipes now," Sarah said. Sarah was simmering molasses and applesauce together to add to the muffin batter.

"My appreciation for your kitchen prowess has certainly increased," Corinne said.

"Thank you, Ma'am," Sarah said.

Because no one was going anywhere, letters and postcards were the primary way of connecting with people. Corinne received a letter from Henrietta about the conditions in London.

Dear Corinne,

How are you? This Spanish flu is ravaging our country. The newspapers first reported it as a secretive sickness from Spain. Now, many hundreds are dying and not just children and older adults. The doctors urge us to employ good hygiene and get fresh air. Schools are closed. There aren't enough doctors and nurses. The only good thing to come of it is that the government has increased our bread rations. I try to walk outside every day. Times are hard, but we must not let this pandemic harden us.

I miss you,

Miggles

To avoid catching the disease, Corinne continued to isolate herself and Sarah at Belmont. She decided to make and send postcards to her friends. She believed that people needed some form of connection amidst the quarantine. She had some old copies of *The Saturday Evening Post,* and she tore up the colored photos. She then used the colored paper to glue collages of rainbows, trees, and flowers to her postcards. She sought anything light to offset the feeling of dread that she had.

Corinne sent one of her postcards back to Henrietta.

> Dear Miggles,
>
> Here are five things I am going to do when the pandemic is over:
>
> 1. Visit and hug my mother.
> 2. Travel.
> 3. Go to a concert.
> 4. Have visitors.
> 5. Smile so someone can see my lipstick without my mask.
>
> I miss you,
>
> Corinne

*

Corinne needed to go to the dentist for a checkup, but elective dental procedures were not allowed. Fear and anxiety overwhelmed Corinne; most of the time, she felt on the verge of tears. As much as she had yearned for a child, in a way, she felt that this was one less thing she had to worry about. As the pandemic droned on, she missed Gari's physical touch. She wasn't out in the world getting handshakes and hugs. She had never really liked crowds, but now that she couldn't go anywhere, she missed them.

Women with cropped hair were all the rage, and Corinne decided to take on the trend as a diversion from all that was going on. She and Sarah pored over her magazines until Sarah was confident she could do the haircut. She hoped that Gari would recognize her when he returned from New York.

Corinne was grateful for her constant companion, Ivy. The loyal animal was never far from her side. She ventured out of the house and walked with Ivy on the garden paths. She used some of her unlimited free time to teach Ivy a few obedience commands.

"Down," she said, and Ivy would drop to the ground.

"Stay," Corinne commanded, and she would walk to the other end of the garden.

"Ivy, come," Corinne directed, and Ivy would fly to her side. Corinne gave her plenty of treats for being so obedient.

"You are such a smart dog," Corinne petted Ivy so enthusiastically that the dog circled around her with her tail wagging.

But all the training that Corinne did could not stop her dog from chewing up paper. Ivy would steal away to her bed in the library with any of Corinne's magazines she could find. Then she would shred them page by page. Many of the women's styles in the Harper's magazines ended up in tatters on the library floor, yet Corinne could not bring herself to punish Ivy. She made the best of the situation by using the paper fragments for more postcards. In times of great turmoil, Corinne was keenly aware she had no control over the world around her; thus, she focused on what she could control to bring herself a sense of grounding.

Corinne worked in her art journal to put her personal feelings on the page. On two facing pages in her journal, she drew an outline of her head and shoulders. She chose to paint the background yellow and the figure in purple on the first page. On the facing page, she painted the background black and the figure yellow. It was very meditative to paint slowly and focus on the figures. The left side symbolized her pandemic-related emotions of feeling drained and overwhelmed. She was nostalgic for the days before the pandemic. She wrote her negative thoughts onto the head of her purple figure in black ink. On the right side, with the yellow figure on the black background, she rendered her positive feelings. She wanted her mind to be rested, sharp, clean, and calm again. She wanted a brave heart again. She wrote these things on the yellow figure. Corinne sat with these two pages for a while and then she wrote "fear" in larger letters on the left-hand side. She wanted to stop fearing her life and fearing this disease. On the right-hand side, she wrote "heal." From the left-hand side to the right-hand side of her journal pages, she felt her negative feelings getting smaller and her positive feelings getting stronger. She thought perhaps they would heal from this pandemic after all, and she could get back to her painting.

*

As much as Corinne eagerly awaited Gari's return from New York in the fall, she realized adjusting to living together again would be challenging. She thought she would feel happiness, but she felt sadness instead. She wanted to put things behind her, but Gari had completely abandoned her during the worst of times. The pandemic had changed her.

Gari tried to appease her upon his return by bringing a pair of bright red rubber boots from New York for Sarah's son, Archie. He rummaged through his suitcases at the front door looking for the boots. "You can give them to him for Christmas," he said without looking up.

Corinne was nervous about him seeing her with her short, bobbed hair for the first time.

"Your hair," Gari said when he cast a look her way. His eyes opened wide in surprise.

"I don't know if that means you like it or you hate it," Corinne said as she plumped up the sides of the cut with her hand.

"I suppose it will just take a little getting used to. But I'm so happy to be back home it doesn't matter what you look like," Gari said, as he lifted his diminutive wife off the ground in a bear hug.

After he dropped her to her feet, Corinne turned away from him for a minute. But then she said, "I like it and I think you're being unkind."

"I didn't mean to come across as unkind, my dear," Gari said. "I do like it."

The couple had to take small steps to rebuild their pre-pandemic bond. They took walks together around Belmont and held hands. She timidly played their favorite tunes on the piano in the parlor.

"I know you're upset with me, but there were things that we could control and things that were beyond our control. I thought it best to stay in New York and work. I thought, 'This too shall pass,'" said Gari. They walked past Corinne's rosebushes and sat on the bench overlooking the river.

"You know I missed you, but I also was a little jealous of you being in New York and me being here. The city must have been so alive, even during the pandemic. I can imagine the sounds of people talking in different languages, firetruck sirens blaring, and children playing.in nearby apartments. You could look out your window and see women dressed in brightly colored dresses and hats, men dressed in their fancy suits. It was so quiet and isolated here," Corinne said.

"There was a high level of isolation there, too. I know you find this hard to believe, but people weren't out and moving about," Gari said.

"Even though I'm still angry at you, I'm happy you're home. For so long, I just wanted to see your smile," Corinne said.

"Well, I'm here to smile for you now. I'm sorry I was gone from you. I want you to feel warm, safe, and loved," Gari said.

"I want to get back to normal as soon as we can," Corinne said as she leaned against Gari's shoulder. He slowly put his arm around her and held her close.

Corinne was thrilled when she saw the huge, six-inch-tall letters on the newspaper's front page on November 11, 1918: "ARMISTICE SIGNED--WAR ENDS AT SIX," it proclaimed. The Terms of the Armistice would be made public later, but for now, the war had ended. It was a ray of sunshine after all the bad news of the pandemic.

Chapter 14

1919: The Detroit Murals

With the war over, Corinne held an Easter party and egg hunt for local children even though the Spanish flu pandemic was still raging in April. She hoped it would be okay since they would be outside and the parents seemed to agree. She loved seeing the children in their Easter finest running here and there in her garden to look for the eggs. It was such a colorful sight. The town needed this small bit of frivolity after the last year.

Some of the younger girls jumped rope and sang the rhyme,

> I had a little bird,
> Its name was Enza.
> I opened the window,
> And in-flew-Enza.

Corinne just shook her head at their antics.

By summer, when people were outside more, the flu deaths subsided. Corinne felt she could travel again. Her mother was now living in Savannah with her older brother, Leonard. She visited in June as her uncle was there to address the Georgia Historical Society on the steamship *Savannah*.

Leonard was an avid book collector and bibliographer. Leonard filled the walls with bookshelves full of colorful, leather-bound books. There were several comfortable reading chairs in the room with Tiffany-stained glass lamps next to them. A rust-colored Oriental rug on the floor made the room feel cozy, and the darkness of the room kept it cool in the summer heat.

After they had settled in for their visit, Corinne remarked, "I just love sitting amongst Leonard's books while we talk, mother." She took a sniff of the air and swore she smelled a hint of vanilla.

"Yes, he has a wonderful collection. I often sit in here and read. I'm very grateful that he didn't have to go to Europe as an interpreter for the war," Louise said.

"I agree. I was so worried about him," Corinne said.

Corinne pulled her chair close to her mother's and held her mother's hand. She had been wanting to do this since the pandemic started.

"What do you think of women getting the right to vote? Women played an essential role in fighting and winning the war. We suffered and sacrificed, just like the men," Corinne said. "It's only right that we have the privilege and right of voting." Corinne followed the news of the suffrage movement and supported it.

"Truth be told, I didn't think I would see it in my lifetime," Louise said. "I always thought that men work, and women stay home to take care of their families."

"You know we're not inferior to men," Corinne said.

"I believe that the Civil War, not the Great War, brought about the right to vote. When all our brave men were off fighting and we women had to take care of the farms and businesses, it changed the way society viewed women's capabilities. Do you think that shift paved the way for future generations of women, like you, to stand up for the rights of citizens and push for suffrage? Women have always stepped up to do what is required of them at the time. Women's participation and work does not mean that they should vote," Louise said.

"I think that women having more education contributed to gaining the right to vote. As we've gained access to higher learning, we've shattered the myth that we're delicate and childlike. We understand complex political issues, economics, and social dynamics just as well as men do. Sometimes even better, given our unique perspectives," Corinne paused before she continued. "We're acutely aware of what's going on in our country, from local matters to national policies. It's become impossible to justify denying us a voice in shaping the very society we're a part of."

"You've always been independent, and I never considered you childlike, even when you were a child."

"Yet, despite our obvious capabilities, most men are still against women voting. They cling to outdated notions of gender roles, fearing what might happen if women had a say in governance, but their resistance only fuels our determination. We've proven ourselves in schools, in workplaces, and in managing households. It's high time our right to participate in democracy is recognized," Corinne said. The intensity of her feelings brought a flush to her cheeks.

"Corinne, this talk is unbecoming of a lady. I did not work so hard to give you a good education so that you could challenge the natural order of things. A woman's place is in the home, not in the voting booth," Louise replied.

"Mother, I understand your concerns," Corinne changed the subject as she felt herself getting riled up. "For now, though, why don't we talk about something we both enjoy."

Louise took a deep breath and her expression softened.

"Speaking of men and perspectives, I've been meaning to ask you. Why didn't Gari join you on this trip? Is everything all right with him?" Louise asked.

"He's always busy with painting and exhibiting," Corinne answered.

"What is your husband painting now?"

"He just finished a quite lovely painting titled *A Young Woman Sewing* and I was the model for it," Corinne said. "It's got pastel blues and pinks painted in the Impressionist style, and the woman looks so serene."

"So, you've resigned yourself to be a model and not a painter?"

"I am still an artist," Corinne said defensively.

"I don't think you'll ever be as accomplished in the art world as your brothers are in their fields. I think you were fortunate that the Salon never accepted your paintings and that you never tried again. Luckily, you married well, and you don't have to be an accomplished artist," Louise said.

Corinne didn't want to continue to argue with her mother after not having seen her for so long, so she let that comment go. She wished her mother was more supportive but asking for acceptance in her family was useless.

Despite her newfound political freedom, Corinne was not painting or making artwork. She wanted to share her creative ideas through painting, but she felt stuck, pulled in many directions. Her mother's comments only added to her self-doubt.

"I'm just feeling stuck," Corinne said to Gari over dinner. She had recently returned from Savannah.

"I may have an answer to that problem," Gari said. "I've received a letter from the architect Cass Gilbert. He is designing a new public library for Detroit. He's asked me to design three murals showing the origins of the city."

"How does that pertain to me?" Corinne asked.

"You know I haven't been feeling well. I have swelling and redness in my legs. It's difficult for me to stand for long periods of time. I'll need help with the preliminary sketches, stretching canvases and finding models. You could help me with all that. Just look at my notebook to see what I've come up with so far." Corinne had noticed that her husband had more gray hair than before. He slouched a little more than he used to. He was not a young man.

She took Gari's notebook into the parlor, sat by the fire, and leafed through it. His sketches of the three murals depicted the settling of Detroit: *The Landing of Cadillac's Wife*, *The Conspiracy of Pontiac,* and *The Spirit of the Northwest.*

The Landing of Cadillac's Wife depicted Detroit's founder Antoine de la Mothe Cadillac embracing his wife as she arrives by boat to the stockade. The arrival of French women showed Detroit as becoming a city and more than just a trapper's outpost.

The Spirit of the Northwest would be the smaller mural, sandwiched in the middle of the other two; it featured a mystical portrayal of Saint Claire with a trapper and a pathfinder on either side of her, representing the spirit of adventure and exploration. The French explorer and fur trader, René-Robert Cavelier, Sieur de La Salle, named a lake in her honor when he explored the Detroit River and the Great Lakes.

The third mural was to be titled *The Conspiracy of Pontiac.* As the leader of several tribes in the region, Chief Pontiac devised a plan to drive the British from the area. He intended to offer the British peace while he entered the fort with concealed weapons to attack the inhabitants. The British learned of the plan and Pontiac backed out. Gari decided to paint the moment when Chief Pontiac offered a wampum belt to the British commander as armed guards stood by.

Gari had come into the parlor and was standing beside her, leaning on his cane, as she finished looking at the sketches.

"How did you come up with these ideas? They're magnificent," Corinne asked.

"Partly, I got the idea from my father. When I was a child, a lumber baron in Detroit named Bela Hubbard commissioned my father to carve four sandstone sculptures of Detroit's four French pioneers. He sculpted Father Jacques Marquette, Sieur de LaSalle, Antoine Cadillac, and Father Gabriel Richard to stand in Detroit City Hall. An interesting pastime for me was looking in the open door of his studio and watching him carve," Gari said.

"You've done your father proud with these sketches. I'm sure the murals will be even better," Corinne said.

"I'm assuming that means you'll help me?" Gari asked, tentatively.

"We will need models for all these subjects. And I'll have to sew costumes for the models," Corinne said. She was already making lists in her head.

"And I'd like you to help with the painting, too. You know my style better than anyone," Gari said.

"Help with the painting, too?" Corinne questioned. "Would they name me as an artist on the project?"

"It doesn't matter if you're named as an artist. The money will still come into this household for the two of us," Gari said. A knot formed in Corinne's stomach at his words, but her excitement for the opportunity to paint outweighed her unease.

Corinne set to the task of helping her husband with the major commission. She invited her younger cousin, McGill Mackall, to stay at Belmont and help with the project, too. McGill was a stained-glass master but also a muralist. They all worked in one of the outbuildings on the property. With Gari's notebook sketches to guide her, she went into Fredericksburg and hired several men and women to model. Then she sewed the costumes. First, she sewed the dresses for the wives of Commander Alphonse Tonty and Antoine Cadillac. Corinne decided to be the model for Cadillac's wife herself. Then she sewed the British guard costume. She put together the trapper, pathfinder, and Pontiac's costumes from clothing she had around the house.

This project was a huge undertaking. After the preliminary pencil sketches in the notebook, the three of them made painted studies of all the characters in color. They drew a grid on each study to ensure that the figures would have the correct proportions and perspective when transferred to the large canvas.

The finished murals were not rectangular but rather had arched tops so that they fit into three arched marble niches in the spacious hall on the second floor of the library.

The citizens of Detroit wanted the murals to tell a story, and Corinne felt they accomplished that goal. They rolled the canvas panels up and traveled by train to Detroit to install them.

While the stone Detroit Museum of Art resembled a medieval castle with two turrets rising on either side, the new Detroit Institute of Arts, built of white marble in an Italian Renaissance style, became a vessel for artwork collected by the city's industry leaders and auto barons.

When they followed the assistants, who were carrying the canvas panels up the stairs to the second floor of the museum, Corinne noticed the children's room. Children clustered around the bright books like bees to honey. The large room was filled with light, tiny tables, and chairs. Glowing tile panels, illustrating fairy tales, were on either side of a fireplace.

"You should be proud of your hometown, Gari. This building is an inspiration." Corinne said to her husband.

"Detroit is the fourth largest city in the United States. I would hope that someday it can have a cultural life at least as unique as New York or Boston," Gari said.

A photographer from the museum took photos of the murals when they were installed. Gari and Corinne stood nearby.

"Mr. Melchers, we'd like to get a photo of you standing in front of your murals," he said.

"Certainly," Gari said as he and Corinne moved to stand next to the mural of the landing of Cadillac's wife.

"If you could step aside, Ma'am. We only want the artist in the photo," the photographer said.

Corinne's face turned bright red as she stepped behind the photographer and watched him take a photo of her husband. She turned away, calmly, attempting to hold in her tears. Gari could hear her footsteps on the marble staircase as she ran downstairs. He had difficulty walking but hobbled after her. He found her in the children's room by the fireplace, fuming.

"Corinne, I had nothing to do with that," Gari said, catching his breath. Corinne whipped around to face him.

"You didn't stand up for me, either. You didn't say that we both worked on the murals," Corinne said.

"But it's my work. It's my reputation. If we want work in the future, this is the way it has to be," Gari said.

Corinne rolled her eyes. Despite not wanting to admit it, she knew he was right. She didn't have the awards that her husband had. She knew in her heart that she was a great artist, but she didn't have credentials to back it up. She also knew that many great artists used artist assistants and fabricators to complete their complex works. The artist assistants always remained anonymous. No one ever commented on the assistants who helped Michelangelo with the Sistine Chapel.

Gari sighed; he loved his wife's spirit. She had been so alive painting the murals, but he vowed to himself he wouldn't ask for her help with his projects again. Extending an invitation was not worth either the tension it brought to their relationship or the pain of rejection that had continually found Corinne. He would work alone, even if the pain in his legs was excruciating.

Chapter 15

1920: London

Gari and Corinne sat in their cheery dining room with its mint green walls, but the mood in the room was anything but lighthearted. Gari noticed Corinne wasn't eating much of her breakfast. She was just pushing the eggs around on the plate.

"Sarah is not going to be happy with you if you don't eat those scrambled eggs," Gari half-heartedly joked with her.

"I'm going to stay with Miggles for a while in London. My cousin McGill will accompany me," Corinne stated without fanfare.

"What's brought this on?" Gari asked. The sharpness in Corinne's tone surprised him.

"I want to work on my painting. I thought that you and I could collaborate, but if you don't give me credit for my work, it's not very satisfying for me," Corinne said.

"Corinne. You know I couldn't tell the architect of the Detroit Public Library, Cass Gilbert, that I had to have my four-foot ten-inch wife help me with those murals. I would've been laughed out of the art world," Gari said.

"The war is over, and women are doing more and more. I'm angry, but I'm trying to not get upset. Sometimes relocation is essential to spark creativity. I thought you of all people would understand that. I thought you would support me," Corinne said. She had tears in her eyes, but she was determined not to cry.

"Go to London if you must. But realize that you can only go because I get paid so much for my paintings," Gari said brusquely. He stood up from the table and stomped out of the room, despite the pain in his legs.

Though her husband had shown flashes of irritation before, today's coldness was something altogether different.

Upstairs in her bedroom, Sarah helped pack her trunk. Corinne also packed a separate bag with her sketchbooks, pencils, paints, and brushes. She sat down at her writing desk and composed a telegram to her friend.

HENRIETTA,

WOULD LIKE TO COME TO LONDON. STOP. NEED SOME TIME TO CONCENTRATE ON MY PAINTING. STOP. MCGILL WILL ACCOMPANY ME. STOP. WILL CONTACT YOU AS SOON AS WE COME ASHORE. STOP. LET ME KNOW IF YOU AGREE. STOP. I WILL WATCH FOR A RESPONSE AS A CAT WATCHES FOR A MOUSE. STOP.

CORINNE.

After a positive reply from Henrietta, Corinne purchased tickets for a stateroom on the Cedric of the White Star Line bound for London. It bothered her she could only get a passport in Gari's name. Although she was traveling alone, without her husband, her passport read Mrs. Gari Melchers.

The ship seemed to roll more than others that Corinne had sailed on. She tried to walk on the deck so that she didn't feel sick in her cabin. She and McGill played a few games of deck quoits. It was an entertaining alternative to shuffleboard, and the on-ship game used rings made of rope so as to not damage the ship's decking.

"Maybe someday we'll be able to fly from New York to London," McGill said. They leaned on the deck railing and looked out across the waves. A flock of seagulls seemed to constantly fly at the stern of the ship.

"I'm sure that will be possible in your lifetime," Corinne answered. "I remember seeing the Zeppelins fly in Germany during the war."

Corinne heard some gulls squawking as the ship neared the dock. A briny smell of mucky sand and stranded shellfish wafted up to her nose. After the uneasy week-long trip, she was happy to depart the ship and head to Henrietta's house.

Corinne and Henrietta hugged as soon as Corinne entered the house. Henrietta planned for Corinne to have a studio a few streets away. She had prepared the studio with an easel and several stretched canvases. She held Corinne's hand as they walked down the cobblestone street near the Thames.

"This is perfect," Corinne said when she stepped over the threshold. A large window opened onto neighboring rooftops. It was a quiet place where Corinne could reflect on her work. Heat rose from the floor grate beneath the window. A wooden easel sat in the center of the space with a small stool.

"I had them put in this chaise lounge, too." Henrietta lay back on the beige couch with roll pillows. "I thought you could use it for your models or for yourself when you get a little tired in the afternoons and want to take a nap."

The first painting that Corinne wanted to do was of her greyhound, Ivy. She missed her so much, but it had been impossible for her to bring her along to London. She had a few photographs of the dog with her. She had never attempted to paint fur, and it was challenging to paint Ivy's brindle coloring. While waiting for the paint to dry between layers, she found herself lost in thought. She found she had to be precise with the brush to capture the fur, and she much preferred to be free and relaxed in her strokes. She progressed from big masses to details. Adding white highlights to Ivy's eyes made her come alive on the canvas, she thought.

Corinne loved watching the mute swans on the Thames as she walked from Henrietta's house to the studio. They were such elegant, magnificent creatures. She picked up a few of their feathers on the way and stuck them in her pocket.

Next, Corinne wanted to revisit still lifes similar to those she had done when trying to get into the Salon. Picking the objects seemed tougher for her. She wanted them to be visually pleasing, but she also wanted them to have something in common. And she wanted them to speak to her. She cut some pink and white hydrangeas from Henrietta's garden, put them in a blue and white vase and took them along to the studio. For added texture and color, she wanted to include other objects. She brought along a coral necklace from Egmondse and thought that the salmon-pink stones would look interesting next to a clear glass. Coral was supposed to bring the wearer luck and perhaps putting coral in her painting would bring her success. Some of her favorite things were in this painting, but it was also technically challenging to paint.

When she finished the painting, she wrote "Still Life with Coral Necklace" on the back. But then, feeling flippant, she signed the painting "C. Lawton" on the front, her mother's maiden name. She was tired of being known as Mrs. Gari Melchers where her art was concerned.

Corinne enjoyed working in her sketchbook after she finished a painting. She didn't like to waste paint, and she didn't want her left-over paint to go into the waterways. Sometimes she just cleaned out her brushes onto an empty page and that became the background. When she had the backgrounds down, she could come back and play with shapes and forms on top. Sometimes she played with the negative space on the page. Sometimes she would draw over a background with some ink. It was a useful tool for sparking ideas. Nobody would see the sketchbook, but it gave Corinne a good feeling. She was happiest in her apron in the studio and would lose track of time. She thought about when she was a young child and all she had wanted to do was draw and paint. Her mother thought her paintings were cute. She didn't discourage her at first, not until Corinne became interested in devoting her life to art. Henrietta or McGill walked to the studio each day to remind her to return for dinner, and they would find her smiling at her thoughts with a paintbrush in her hand.

At dinner, Corinne enjoyed discussions with her best friends, Miggles and Charles. In 1920, Charles was in the midst of writing a novel, *The Enchanted Stone.*

"I want to hear all about your book," Corinne passed the mashed potatoes around the table. When she set the bowl down, she inadvertently knocked over her glass of wine, soaking the tablecloth.

"I'm so sorry," Corinne apologized.

"Not a problem. I'll get the girl to clean it up," Miggles said. Her maid rushed in from the kitchen and dabbed at the wine stain on the tablecloth. Corinne thought about Sarah back at home at Belmont. There was a time she would have acted in exactly the same manner as her friend. But after their closeness during the pandemic, she would never call Sarah, "the girl." Corinne shook her head at the thought. Soon, Corinne had a fresh glass of wine.

"Now that we have cleaned up my mess, back to your book," Corinne said.

"It's a romance of the most curiously fantastic sort. I have invented an enchanted stone, stolen from an East Indian temple. A certain brotherhood of Indians is scouring the world to find and recover it. These brothers are entertainingly tattooed on their arms with symbolic characters, and they have a mysterious meeting place in London. They secure the aid of a billionairess who undertakes to build them a new temple. She employs a half-crazy architect, who is also entertaining in a bizarre fashion, to build it. And finally, the entire story becomes a mince pie dream," Charles said.

"You say the Indians have symbols tattooed on their arms, I've seen women lately as I walk back and forth from the studio who have blush for cheeks, color for lips, and even their eyeliner tattooed on," Corinne said.

"A new trend in makeup for the upper classes," Henrietta said.

"Charles, your story sounds like a queer riddle or puzzle," Corinne said.

"It is interesting and will do if one has time to read it. Stories such as mine sometimes provide answers of a kind and sometimes leave you to mull the ideas over on your own," Charles said, sipping from his glass of wine.

"I will make time to read it while I'm here," Corinne said.

Even though Corinne was angry with Gari, she still missed him while she was in London. He was the first thing she thought about when she woke in the morning and the last thing she thought about before she fell into sleep each night. She wanted to lay her head against his chest and listen to his heartbeat. In her mind, she pictured gazing into his deep gray eyes. She wondered if he missed her at all.

While Corinne was gone, Gari stayed at Belmont and painted many views from the house. He enjoyed looking out over the Rappahannock River and recreating the idyllic scenes of the cows in the pasture below.

He went to the Fredericksburg Fairgrounds and snapped photographs of the horse races. He returned to Belmont and painted the scene. He included a little joke for his neighbors in Stafford as he listed them on the tote board in the infield as the jockeys.

My dear Peachy,

I'm sitting at my easel in the studio yet again, thinking of you. How I miss your beautiful face and how I wish you were here with me. I've only recently realized how much painting I do, and I think I finally understand why you had to go to London. The house is so lonely and quiet without you. I miss hearing you play the piano. When you return (not if, when) I will do what I can to ensure that you paint every day.

Last week I visited the fairgrounds and took some photos of the horse races. I've been painting a composite scene, but I don't have the desire to finish it. I used our neighbors' names on the tote board--Brooks, Humphrey, Payne, Gibbs, and Donovan. I even placed our grounds man, Mr. Dillon in the number one slot. Do you think they'll get a kick out of that kind of joke?

I miss you so much. I can't wait to see you. I love you more than anything.

Yours,

Mr. M

Corinne, though not due to his unamusing joke, thought it was time for her to return to Belmont. She missed having all her animals around her, and she missed her husband after almost a year away from him.

Chapter 16

1921: Richmond

Corinne asked Miggles and Charles to accompany her back to Belmont. McGill came along, too. A year in London had been enough time for Corinne to reignite her creativity. They arrived in time to prepare the house for New Year's Eve and held a French-style country dance. Corinne invited three soldier musicians from Quantico to play. Seated at the parlor's piano, they looked dashing in their uniforms.

"Miggles, will you help me with my dress? I made it last summer, but it's just not right," Corinne asked.

Henrietta worked on the velvet blue dress for two days and then helped Corinne with the fitting.

"This dress makes your eyes shine, but are you sure you won't be too uncomfortable wearing it? It's quite warm here for a January day," Henrietta said.

"No, I'll be fine. Gari will love me in it," Corinne winked. Corinne felt guilty about the time spent away from her husband and wanted to please him.

The dance drew about eighty guests, including neighbors ranging in age from seven to seventy-eight. Corinne thought it was quite a success, except for Gari's awkwardness. He had avoided talking to Corinne the whole evening. How could he still be so cold?

On their way up the stairs to bed, Corinne reached out and took Gari's hand. He held her hand tentatively.

"You might have thought I was wrong to go to London, but I learned so much about myself while there. I know I hurt you, but coming back home feels right," Corinne said.

"I'm happy you're home, my dear. You look beautiful this evening. And I hope we can learn from our separation and put it behind us," Gari said.

The next day, they sat around the table in the dining room and quietly chatted, read, and wrote while a fire crackled behind them. The turning of book pages was the most prevalent sound in the room. It was a relaxed, simple New Year's Day after the party the evening before. While they sat in the dining room, Gari showed Corinne a letter.

*

Corinne was invited to meet Judge John Barton Payne. He was the executive head of the American Red Cross, and Corinne had impressed him with her volunteer activities for the organization during the war. She travelled to Washington, DC for their meeting.

"You simply must come to Belmont, your Honor. I've just returned home there from a trip to London, and I enjoy it more each time I see it," Corinne said as she and Judge Payne left the meeting.

"Call me John," Judge Payne said. "I'm thrilled that you moved to Virginia. I've been a Fauquier County man my whole life, no matter where I've lived."

"My husband and I enjoy Falmouth and Fredericksburg very much," Corinne said.

"I will come to Belmont. But before I do, I'd like you and your husband to make the brief trip to Richmond as my guests and attend the opening of the Confederate Memorial Institute," Payne said.

"We would be honored," Corinne said. Back at Belmont, the invitation soon arrived in the mail.

In May, Gari and Corinne joined five-hundred people attending the opening of the art exhibit donated by Payne to the Confederate Memorial Institute in Richmond. The building also housed a large, four-panel mural by Charles Hoffbauer featuring Confederate generals on horseback. Many of the visitors were Confederate veterans and women from the South. Gari and Corinne took their seats on the patio.

The Confederate Memorial Institute was given the nickname "Battle Abbey." The United Confederate Veterans built Battle Abbey to hold statuary, portraits, flags, books, and manuscripts relating to Confederate history. The name came from Virginian Charles Baltzall, or "Broadway" Rouss. He was a Richmond merchant who joined the cavalry in 1864, but the war had left him destitute. He scraped together meager funds to open a shop in New York City that grew into a nationwide franchise. With his new wealth, he wanted to leave a legacy and offered $100,000 to veteran and memorial organizations to build a dedicated place to save Confederate relics of the war.

A sea of gray-haired white men in their battle grays and slouch hats surrounded Gari and Corinne. There was a faint odor of lanolin from the sea of wool. Corinne leaned over to an elderly man seated next to her.

"You look quite dashing in your uniform," she said.

"Thank you, Ma'am. I'm just happy it still fits me after all these years. I'm in my eighties now. Major General Walker B. Freeman, commander of the United Confederate Veterans' Virginia Division, asked that any veterans attending should do so in uniform. He's going to be speaking today," the man replied through a semi-toothless smile.

General Walker approached the dais to a rousing round of applause.

"Let us show our appreciation of the importance and historic meaning of this occasion, and at the same time enjoy the privilege and pleasure of seeing the artistic beauties of this sacred shrine, dedicated to the perpetual memory of the Southern Confederacy," General Walker said to the crowd.

Several hundred members of the John Marshall High School girls chorus sang Confederate songs for the occasion, "Bonnie Blue Flag," "Maryland," and "Dixie." The high school cadet band played patriotic tunes to entertain the guests. Gari and Corinne applauded along with the others. As Gari and Corinne were getting up from their chairs, they ran into Judge Payne in the crowd.

"The Melchers. So glad you could make it. How great to see you," Judge Payne said as he shook Gari's hand.

"Thank you for the invitation, Sir," Gari said.

"Have you been inside yet?" Judge Payne asked.

"No, not yet. We've been enjoying the program," Gari answered.

"Please, come inside," Judge Payne beckoned with an open arm towards the door.

"I have donated my art collection of fifty paintings and two busts to the state—one of Benjamin Franklin, sculpted by Hiram Powers, and one of Sir Isaac Newton—in memory of my dear second wife, Jennie Byrd Bryan," the judge continued.

"That was very generous of you, Sir," Gari said.

"No need to be so formal. Call me John," Judge Payne said. As the three of them walked through the gallery, they looked at the paintings hung haphazardly in Battle Abbey.

"It's not really a suitable building for an art collection," Corinne whispered in Gari's ear.

At the conclusion of the ceremony, Corinne asked Gari if they could visit some parts of Richmond before they returned home. They took a trolley to an area called Libby Hill Park in Church Hill, stopping to take in the view. Behind them was the Confederate Soldiers and Sailors Monument; it was so tall that it towered over them. It was a bronze statue of a Confederate private atop a pillar composed of thirteen granite blocks to symbolize each of the Confederate states. The park had several fountains and winding cobblestone paths on the hillside. The James River snaked around a bend in the valley below them. To their right were rows upon rows of tobacco warehouses.

"Look at this view," Corinne said. "Here's a plaque about it." She read the words aloud: 'The curve of the James River and steep slope on this side are very much like the features of the River Thames in England, a royal village west of London called Richmond Upon Thames. In the early 1730s, William Byrd II, an important planter, merchant, politician, and writer, was asked by the House of Burgesses to plan a town at the Falls of the James in the early 1730s. As he had traveled several times to Richmond Upon Thames, it is believed that the view led him to name this new town 'Richmond.'"

Gari harrumphed. Although he said that he was happy to have their separation behind them, he still wasn't over the fact that Corinne had gone to London on her own.

"Miggles and I were at this area of London where the Thames makes this turn," Corinne said.

"I wouldn't know anything about that, having not been in London as recently as you," Gari said as he waved his cane at the view of the river.

"Let's get back to Belmont," Corinne said to avoid an argument. She did not want to rile Gari up.

Once back at home, they were met with some disturbing news. While they were away in Richmond, Ivy had gotten away from Sarah.

"She slipped past me when I opened the door, ma'am. She was across the field afore I could even call for her. She must have been chasin' a rabbit. I'm terribly sorry," Sarah said with her head bowed.

Corinne was heartsick that Ivy was gone.

"Sarah, how could you? We must find her. I'll put an advertisement in the Free Lance-Star," Corinne said, and she did.

It read:

"STRAYED. A greyhound with brindle markings. Last seen in Falmouth, going North. Reward. Mrs. Gari Melchers."

Ivy had already been gone for two days. Corinne pulled on her wellies and started searching for her immediately. She recruited a few of her neighbors to help. Corinne felt Ivy was still upset with her for having gone away to London. Gari wasn't the only one who was perturbed that she had been gone.

"Bring along your dogs. That might entice her to come closer. But don't chase her if you see her. That will just cause her to run farther," Corinne said to the search party. The group started off near the river, where Ivy was last seen. Luckily, Corinne had taught Ivy to come when called. She hoped that would benefit her now.

"Ivy. Come!" Corinne called out as she and her neighbors walked across the field.

Corinne thought she saw a patch of brown under a bush next to a fence. She moved in that direction. Ivy was hiding there and must have been there for several days.

"Who's a good girl?" Corinne said as she knelt next to the cowering dog. Ivy jumped up from her hiding place, almost into Corinne's arms. Corinne slipped a leash over her head and walked Ivy back to the house as quickly as she could. Ivy went straight to her water bowl as soon as she entered the house.

"Please get her something to eat, Sarah," Corinne said. Ivy wolfed down the food in the bowl. "She has a few scrapes and is a little thinner than normal, but I think she will be fine."

Sarah heaved a sigh of relief. "I won't let it happen again, ma'am," she said.

"I certainly hope not," Corinne said sternly.

In July, Corinne was pleased to see her cousin, McGill, when he came to Belmont with his fiancé to visit from Baltimore. After spending so much time together in London, McGill and Corinne were close, and he wanted his aunt to meet his fiancé, Harriet Strode.

Corinne took the visitors in their new motorcar along Route 3 through lush farmlands to Potomac Beach for a picnic. They spread a blanket on the riverbank. Corinne undid the leather straps and opened the wicker basket; fried chicken wrapped in paraffin paper, cheese sandwiches with the cheese grated and moistened with cream, a couple of sliced cucumbers from the gardens at Belmont, and peach pie for dessert. Corinne brought along lemons and sugar to make some lemonade, along with a thermos bottle of cool water.

"Just walking to the picnic spot made me hungry," McGill said.

"It is a beautiful day to spend a day out in the open with the sky over our heads. I love being by the river," Corinne said.

They lounged under Shady sycamore trees, which provided some relief from the scorching sun. After they finished lunch, Corinne and McGill sat on the blanket while Harriet searched for a place to discard the leftovers from the picnic.

"She's a beautiful girl, McGill. I'm excited about your marriage. Do you think you will have many children?" Corinne asked.

"I'd love to have a house full," McGill said with a smile. The smile then faded. "I always wondered why you and Gari never had any children."

"It just wasn't to be," Corinne answered. "I know that Gari always wanted children, and we had enough money to raise children. He made it so obvious by all those paintings he made of mothers and their babes. It has always haunted me a little every time I look at one of those paintings that I couldn't give him children."

"But you know, Gari has traveled frequently, going back and forth to his studio in New York City. It would have been hard on a child for him to be away so much," McGill said.

"It would have meant some sacrifice and compromise on his part," Corinne said. "And those are things he isn't used to making."

They watched as Harriet returned from her search. Her light skirt fluttered in the breeze.

"On a lighter note, I do hope there aren't many mosquitoes out today," McGill said.

The three of them waded ankle deep into the Potomac. "We also have to watch out for stinging jellyfish," Corinne said. "The biting insects distract me from looking at the birds, too. Look! There's a great blue heron over there in the shallows. Isn't it magnificent?"

"Yes, it's beautiful," Harriet said. The heron flew off when they approached.

"It's kind of a slate gray rather than blue, isn't it? That long, sinuous neck and dagger-like bill. It looks like a prehistoric dinosaur when it flies. When we return to our picnic blanket, I'll make a quick sketch of it," Corinne said.

"You have always loved birds, haven't you?" McGill observed.

"Maybe I shall try to paint the great heron when we are back at Belmont," Corinne said. She had gained a renewed love of painting after her time in London.

Chapter 17

1923: The Art Critic

"We must build a studio here so that we both can work," Gari said. "It would be so much easier to entertain clients here than in New York. Especially with the pain in my legs from the phlebitis. The burning. The swelling. Some days I can barely walk. And I want the studio to be for both of us, so you don't run off to London again."

"How about a studio built from stone?" Corinne asked.

On the property were the remains of a stone bridge dynamited by Union forces during the Civil War; fieldstone was also abundant, left from houses destroyed in nearby battles. The Melchers had a studio constructed from the stone with a roof of slate. A large window allowed them both to paint by a northern exposure. Gari installed his workbench, easel, and two Dutch wardrobes. Corinne hung his medals and awards for achievement on the walls. They had the Melchers family coat of arms carved onto the studio's exterior. They hung a massive chandelier in the middle of the room, but there was still plenty of room to paint and display the large paintings and murals that Gari was known for. His cozy chair sat in front of the easel.

Corinne had a smaller desk and easel at the opposite end of the room. She also liked to sketch outside on the grounds of Belmont. She now had a new studio on the Belmont property in which she could paint for hours every day.

For Valentine's Day that year, Gari surprised Corinne with a Secret Lace Heart. It was a new Valentine's Day gift introduced by the Russell Stover Chocolate Company. A heart-shaped box covered in satin and black lace and filled with a variety of their best chocolates.

"Some sweets for my sweet," Gari said.

Corinne took one of the chocolate-covered cherries from the box and bit into it. She tilted her head back to keep the cherry liquid from squirting out. Gari wiped some of the cherry juice from the side of her mouth as it dribbled out.

"It's heavenly. After I eat the chocolates, I'm going to keep this beautiful box for your love letters," Corinne said. Her feelings toward her husband had softened in the three years since she'd returned from her year in London.

As a surprise for Gari's Valentine's Day gift, Corinne made ice cream for him. She asked Mr. Dillon to retrieve some ice chunks from the river and carry them up to the house. She smashed the chunks into small pieces putting them, along with some rock salt, into the wooden ice cream maker. Inside of it was a metal bucket where she placed cream, sugar, and a teaspoon of vanilla. She spent hours turning the handle back and forth, stopping every so often to scrape down the sides of the bucket where the ice cream formed. It was easy to start with and then got harder and harder as the ice cream stiffened.

"What a special surprise!" Gari exclaimed when he saw what Corinne was doing on the front porch. She was bundled up in her winter coat, scarf, and gloves.

"You like ice cream, and I enjoy making ice cream. It all works out," Corinne said.

"If this is the result of getting you that box of chocolates, I believe I will get one for you every year from now on," Gari said.

Corinne smiled as she turned the crank one more time.

In March, Gari left Belmont to install four murals in Jefferson City, Missouri. For this project, he did not ask for Corinne's help as he thought it safer for their relationship. He asked McGill to join him instead, as McGill had helped him with the Detroit murals. Gari decided to send his wife love letters while he was away.

Corinne stayed at Belmont and busied herself with planting six elms to the east of the house. She wanted a shady spot near the stone horseshoe staircase to sketch or to walk with Ivy on hot summer days. She also worked on tending her rose garden ; it was so hot and humid in Virginia, roses didn't grow well, but that didn't stop Corinne from experimenting with different plants. She tried Swamp Roses and Pasture Roses in beds around the house. In the mornings, she stooped over the rose bushes to dead head the blooms; their fragrances filled the new day's air. She enjoyed watching the large bumblebees buzzing from flower to flower.

Gari was proud of the murals for Missouri. The most striking was his portrait of Mark Twain, whom he painted wearing a white suit in the pilothouse of a Mississippi river steamer. Next to Twain, a uniformed pilot moves the enormous steering wheel with his hand and foot. Twain's suit is in marked contrast to the blues of the sky and of the pilot's uniform.

The famous children's poet, Eugene Field, was his next subject. Gari painted him in his usual careless dress, casually sitting on a table in his study. A young, tow-headed boy plays near him on the floor with his toy soldiers. With blue tones throughout the painting, Gari staged the scene as an illusion to Field's poem "Little Boy Blue."

The third panel shows Miss Susan Blow of St. Louis in the interior of what likely was the first American kindergarten. She wears an old-fashioned, rose-colored dress in tune with the period. She stands in front of a blackboard; one little girl clings to her teacher's dress and another holds a doll. The blackboard is adorned with drawings of Froebel's theory that play is the expression of a child's soul and the words "Let Us Live for the Children."

The last painting, marked with tones of green and brown, shows Major James S. Rollins, the founder of Missouri State University, standing in front of the university campus with a cape thrown over his shoulder. One of the university's original buildings is featured in the background.

They installed the paintings in the Governor's Reception Room of the Capitol Building. The grand room was shaped as an ellipse and faced the river. The paintings were framed in four large panels, covering half of the room. Above the works was a frieze of solid oak bearing carvings of seals representing the states of the Union. Like the murals for the Detroit Public Library, these murals were painted on heavy canvas and then attached to the plaster walls with white lead; with this technique, Gari's works became part of the wall itself.

At the installation and unveiling, Gari remarked to an attendee next to him, "I was struck by the dilapidated appearance of the farms and towns in Illinois and Indiana. But then how much better they appeared between St. Louis and Jefferson City." The man laughed in agreement.

Major Rollins' son was present at the installation. "The portrait of my father is such a close likeness. It's almost as if he's standing in front of me," he said to Gari.

"Thank you. This setting for the murals surpasses even what I was expecting. My own father would be so proud of my paintings under that frieze," Gari said.

"I'm sure your father would be proud," the younger Rollins said.

"It took me the better part of a year to paint these. Of course, I used photographs rather than models, or it would have taken longer. My studio at Belmont was not quite finished, so I painted them in New York. Seeing them hanging here is just remarkable; I hope that someday I can bring my wife to see them—she is an artist, too," Gari said.

"Well, if she's an artist, she would enjoy them just as much as we do," Rollins said.

"Corinne would love them," McGill agreed.

*

In April, Gari had an exhibition at the Baltimore Museum of Art. *The Baltimore Sun* critiqued the exhibition in an article written by James McNeill Whistler's ghost.

"James McNeill Whistler—in the spirit—walked through the galleries at the April opening of the Baltimore Museum of Art last night. The exhibition impressed him, perhaps, as follows:

> First, I will talk about my own things. They are very nice, indeed. I see they have 'The Nocturne' from the 'Venice Set.' Which is admirable.
>
> It is amusing to recall the reception this same 'Venice Set' received in London when I brought it back with me from pleasant Italy. The so-called critics termed the etchings 'mere sketches,' 'simply memoranda,' and 'all to be developed later.'
>
> Charming and naïve in their asininity, were they not? Mere sketches—which will live as long as the universe spins around. Memoranda—which will furnish the tenth

generation with artistic inspiration. To be developed later—what?—perfection knows no development.

But, to revert as I should to this review, here they all are in Baltimore. Baltimore, where I once lived. My father was a civil engineer for the Baltimore and Ohio railroad. And, further, the excellence of my exhibition speaks eloquently for the artistic resource of Baltimore.

They have my 'The Kitchen,' really one of the best things I ever did. 'The Lime Burner' is also there, as it should be—a charming thing that. Many, many more—53 in all, I believe.

My superb impression 'La Salute Dawn,' which is given, reminds me of the bustling old lady who once stood with me before it. Said the bustling old lady, after close examination of the masterpiece:

'But Mr. Whistler, I have never seen a dawn like that.'

All I could reply was: 'Don't you wish you could, Madam?'

All this, however, is getting a bit too self-centered, even for Jamie McNeill, I'm afraid. Let us continue around the galleries.

Gari Melchers is exhibited. Unfortunately, he was born in Detroit, Mich. From the printed announcement, I notice his masterpieces are gathered from such splendid centers of American art as Youngstown, Savannah, Buffalo, Minneapolis, and the master's own Detroit.

Faced with such territorial eminence, I dare not be too harsh. I can only say that Melchers is a frightened Zuloago painting with his left hand.

In concluding these remarks, I ask those who are to be fortunate enough to visit the Museum of Art during this exhibition—I ask them to see my etchings last of all. If this is not done, the other things will appear miserably shallow."

The critique was a scathing one for Gari. Corinne was furious when she read the review in the newspaper.

"How can he say such things about you? Zuloago was a great Spanish painter with realistic subject matter. I thought that you, Whistler, and Sargent were all friends," Corinne said.

"It's not Whistler who is saying it. It is the art critic from *The Baltimore Sun*. You know I paint all kinds of subjects. Portraits, landscapes, nudes, still lifes. I paint in watercolor and oil. I don't fit in a standard box for these critics," Gari said.

"But you speak to people through your art. You remind people of scenes and stories they know. I don't understand how critics can't see that," Corinne said.

"Come outside in the spring sunshine and let's leave the critics for another day," Gari said. They walked out onto the grounds of Belmont where the cherry trees were blossoming. Around the terraces, the daffodils and hyacinths were blooming and filled the air with a sweet honey-like fragrance that captured the essence of early spring. They sat on the bench overlooking the Rappahannock River and took in the green Virginia hillside.

Corinne felt calmer. As much as she was vying for recognition from the art world at large for her own talent, she also wanted to champion her husband's work. She wanted the outside world to acknowledge him for his efforts. He was just as accomplished an artist as Sargent, Whistler, or Chase; in fact, the three artists acknowledged Gari's significant contributions to figurative and realistic art, believing that Gari had developed his own style of naturalism.

Chapter 18

1925: Barbados

Corinne's mother passed away on August 26, 1925. The obituary mentioned Louise "Lulu" Lawton Mackall, but Corinne did not know many people who referred to her mother by that name. Louise Mackall had been ill for several months and had lived the remainder of her life with her eldest son, Leonard, in Savannah. Her brother, Lawton, arrived first from New York. Corinne followed from Virginia.

After the funeral procession left Leonard's home and the body was delivered to the church, the priest delivered a Requiem High Mass. Louise laid in a flower covered casket; a large cross, compiled of roses and carnations, was next to her. The sub deacon sang "Beautiful Land on High" and "Some Sweet Day."

Deep grief etched the children's faces as their mother's coffin was lowered into the grave. Father Duffy conducted the committal service. People fanned themselves in the heat with the paper fans the funeral home provided them. Corinne had traveled from Fredericksburg in her black mourning clothes. The paper fans were not enough relief for her, and she passed out next to the grave in the Georgia heat.

"Mother will live in the hearts she left behind," her brother Lawton said, as he knelt beside Corinne and patted her hand. She reached for his arm so he could help her get up. The other mourners gathered around her. She unsteadily took some steps toward the hearse.

"Let's just go back to Leonard's house," Corinne said. She didn't enjoy being the center of attention on a day that should be devoted to her mother's memory. "I think I'd like to lie down for a while."

Corinne knew that her mother hadn't approved of her becoming an artist, or of her quick marriage to a man who was twenty-two years her senior. After her mother's funeral, Corinne returned to Belmont and she had trouble sleeping. She missed her mother more than she realized she would. She sat on the cream-colored settee in the parlor and stared off into space. Sometimes she didn't get out of bed and Gari could hear her crying.

As if Corinne's mother passing wasn't enough, a few weeks after she returned from Georgia, Corinne's beloved Ivy passed away, too. She had been ill with some stomach problems that only seemed to worsen while Corinne was away. Corinne wrapped her body in a homemade blanket and buried her next to the rosebushes at Belmont. If anyone ever found her bones, the tattered blanket would tell them that this hound had been loved.

Afterwards, Corinne could sometimes sense Ivy around Belmont. She often thought that she'd seen her out of the corner of her eye. One morning, Corinne glanced up from the sofa and thought she saw Ivy passing into the dining room. But it was Gari standing in the doorway.

"I have a surprise for you," he said at breakfast one morning. "I know you've been feeling sad without your mother and Ivy. I'm sixty-five years old now myself, and who knows how much longer I'll be around. So, I think we should go on a tropical vacation."

"Where to?" Corinne asked.

"The island of Barbados. Tropical beaches. Blue Caribbean water. Sea turtles and flying fish. I think it will take your mind off things here," Gari answered.

"Hmmm," Corinne made a sound that wasn't quite an approval. Part of her did like the idea of getting away for a while.

Corinne and Gari sailed from New York City to Bridgetown. When they arrived at their hotel, they took in the spectacular views of the harbor and the ocean. Wild green monkeys, with thick coats of brown highlighted with yellows and greens, were all over the island. Corinne loved watching them, and they lifted her spirits. Their expressions and antics captivated her. She watched as one bounced across the lawn of the hotel with a banana in its hand; nearby, another monkey swung through the trees. Corinne wanted to paint them, but she didn't quite have the strength or will to do it yet.

While in Barbados, Gari painted, and Corinne sunned herself on the beach. It had been hot at her mother's funeral, but the heat on this island was much deeper. She loved walking all alone, barefoot on the soft, white sand beaches. And she had never seen water of such a beautiful aqua color. She had heard that Cattlewash Beach, where they were located, had healing properties, but sometimes, while walking on the beach, she would feel overwhelmed and cry. She felt disconnected, as though her life was happening to someone else.

Gari painted numerous paintings of the local people and the boats in the harbor. He used gouache so that the paintings would dry quickly. The local Bajan people appreciated his smile and loved to talk about their island to him while he painted them. He painted a muscular, barefoot young man in *A Harbor Boy* and a barefoot woman crowned with a red turban in *Ma Petite*.

They ate delicious pink grapefruit for breakfast and flying fish and cou cou for dinner, an okra and cornmeal dish they had never tasted before. Open windows in the dining room let in the sea breezes. Sometimes a monkey would gaze at them during dinner. Gari would reach for Corinne's hand when he saw her smile at the monkey.

"I can see that we might be descended from monkeys, as Mr. Scopes tried to teach his class. Look at that mother over there, shaking her head 'no' at her little one. He's playing with his food, and she wants him to eat it," Corinne said.

"I'm not sure William Jennings Bryan would agree with you. And having painted many mothers and babies, I'm not sure I agree with you," Gari said.

"Perhaps you should paint a monkey family portrait," Corinne joked half-heartedly.

Gari gazed at Corinne across the table. She wasn't completely over her mother's death, but she was coming back.

Gari had seen a beautiful red macaw in the marketplace while he was out painting and purchased it while Corinne was back in their room. He had thought about getting her another puppy or even a small monkey after he had seen how much she loved watching the monkeys on the island, but he decided she would love the bird more.

"I want you to wear this blindfold," Gari said. Surprised, Corinne looked up from her tea and allowed him to adjust the scarf around her eyes.

"Take my hand and follow me," Gari said. He led Corinne from the breakfast nook in the restaurant onto the patio of their hotel room. Corinne tilted her head as she heard a trill followed by a whistle.

"What is that?" she asked. Gari removed the blindfold, and there, in a golden cage, was the most beautiful scarlet Macaw parrot. Corinne slowly reached into the cage and took the parrot onto her wrist. With its long tail feathers, the parrot was nearly the same height as Corinne.

"It's a gift. For you. You can teach her to talk," Gari said.

"How many words do you think a parrot can learn?" Corinne asked. She beamed, obviously pleased with her gift. Gari kissed her sweetly.

"I'm not sure, but I think she already loves to sing," Gari said as the parrot gurgled and whistled in some kind of song. The parrot also made many clicking sounds.

Corinne returned her to her perch and watched the bird hop around the cage. "I'm going to name her Polly. We'll tell stories together, sing together, and maybe even dance together."

With the parrot in tow in a gilded cage, Gari and Corinne returned to Belmont. Corinne wasted no time talking to Sarah about Polly.

"You must be extremely careful cleaning around her cage. You can't use anything harsh," Corinne explained.

"Yes, ma'am," Sarah said. "May I use the broom around her? Or will that scare her?"

"You don't have to tiptoe around her. She shouldn't be nervous about that. But birds bite. Don't stick your finger in the cage," Corinne said.

"Yes, ma'am," the housekeeper said obediently. "I'll leave gettin' her outa the cage to you."

Days flowed into weeks with the parrot, and Corinne slowly emerged from her grief. Polly sat on the wooden frame on the back of the sofa at Belmont, and Corinne handed her a playing card to chew. Then she thought better of it and went upstairs to her writing desk to retrieve some plain index cards. She placed these around the living room. Polly inched towards one of the index cards, but then stopped and looked at Corinne. Corinne could see that she was trying to decide whether she was allowed to chew the index card.

"I wanna try it?" Polly asked.

"Okay." Corinne said. Polly then picked up the index card and chewed. Polly reminded Corinne of her dear Ivy. At least she chewed blank index cards and not Corinne's copies of *Harper's Magazine.*

Later in the evening, Polly rubbed her head against Corinne. "Good night bird," Polly said. Polly always said good night to herself. Corinne put her back in her cage and covered it with a cloth.

A few months after returning from Barbados, and with the distraction of Polly, Corinne became her old self again. She ate her breakfast in the dining room as Gari read *The Free Lance Star* newspaper, something she hadn't done routinely for a long time, but now, on an ordinary Tuesday morning in October, they seemed to have returned to their normal life.

"Look at this," Gari said as he showed Corinne an advertisement. "We can go to DC on the train to watch the Washington Senators play in the World Series against the Pittsburgh Pirates."

"Since when did you become interested in baseball?" Corinne asked.

"I thought a baseball game might offer some interesting scenes to paint," Gari said.

"Perhaps," Corinne said.

Gari folded the newspaper in half and slid it across the table to Corinne. "It says here that the Senators have a player named Joe Harris. His nickname is 'The Moon.' He's been playing great in the Series. In Game 4 he hit two home runs. There's almost nothing they can pitch to him that he can't hit. I would like to paint his portrait."

"We'll see. Maybe the trip to Barbados was enough traveling for me," Corinne said as she took a sip of her coffee. Gari's excitement about seeing a game waned with her comment.

As Christmas approached, Corinne planned a puppet show for the local children and made all the puppets herself. She threw herself wholeheartedly into the project; she especially liked the puppet she made of Polly.

Corinne decided to make her puppet show a version of Jack and the Beanstalk, but instead of a hen that laid golden eggs, she had her Polly puppet play that role. She made puppets of Jack, his mother, the giant, the giant's wife, and the bean seller. She fashioned the bean seller after the man in the marketplace where she had gotten her first dog, Luek. Jack resembled a young Gari. Corinne painted several tableaux as backdrops for the story. She sewed curtains for a small stage and placed the stage in the foyer of Belmont. She sent out invitations to her Yuletide Festival to the local school, scheduling different classes to attend on each day of the event. After every performance, the children erupted in enthusiastic applause. Their gleeful laughs filled Corinne with such joy.

Corinne drew and titled her own Christmas cards. "A Bountiful Christmas to You" featured a cornucopia of gifts falling from the sky. $1,000 bills, a baby in a cradle, flowers, champagne, and a French horn. She based her card, "Blessed Christmas," on one of their antique wax figurines of the Holy Family's flight into Egypt. Her neighbors and friends anticipated seeing what she would draw on the cards each year. Many of them collected the cards and saved them for their own decorations.

Corinne also celebrated Christmas by baking. She didn't trust Sarah to bake the fruitcakes, although it was Sarah who had taught her to bake during the pandemic. She gifted two kinds of fruitcakes to her friends and neighbors, one with coconut and almonds and the other with molasses and allspice. The house filled with the spicy aromas. Corinne knew that her mother would have loved to see her baking… and not painting. Nevertheless, she had decided she was finished replaying her mother's criticism and hurtful remarks in her head. She was finally at peace with herself.

Chapter 19

1926: Philadelphia Sesqui-Centennial

Gari began the new year with a show at the Anderson Galleries in Brooklyn. The New York Society of Artists invited Gari to become a member, and the show at the Anderson Galleries in Brooklyn served as an introduction. His work of Mrs. John W. Garrett in a Spanish costume was given a conspicuous place in the largest gallery, a space preserved for the picture of honor in the show. His portrait stood out with its colors of white, black, and crimson against a greyish background. The Garretts were from Baltimore. John was a diplomat and both he and his wife, Alice, supported the arts.

At the opening, Gari and Corinne surveyed the other paintings in the show. They walked through the galleries arm in arm. Corinne wore a flat blue crepe dress featuring a swagger tie collar and a button trimmed drop waist. Gari wore a Piccadilly-style blue cashmere suit. It had wide shoulders tapering at the waist and wide, straight trousers. The artwork nearly had to compete with the couples' attire.

"I'm not particularly happy with this show. Not all these painters and sculptors are at their best," Gari said.

"There are some weak spots in the show," Corinne agreed. "But Mrs. Garrett's portrait is very strong. It's stunning."

"And I do like that they hung my *The Girl in Blue* and *Homework* paintings next to it," Gari said.

"The painters in this show are modern, but they are not freakish in their desire to show that they are ultra-modern. Salvador Dali, Max Ernst, and René Magritte, with their surrealist paintings, are not showing up here," Corinne said.

"In this new year, I want to use my paintings to let go of the previous year and call new experiences into our lives. But I will never paint in the Surrealist style. That's just not me," Gari said.

"I don't care to paint in the Surrealist style either. And I want to let go of the previous year, as well," Corinne agreed, However, she had other reasons for letting go.

After her mother's death the year before, Corinne thought she might throw herself into committee work around Fredericksburg where she could use her creativity. Not only did she grieve her mother's death, but she also longed for her past self. She wanted to draw and paint again. Expressing her creativity supported her health and well-being.

In the summer, Philadelphia held a fair to celebrate the one hundred and fiftieth anniversary of the signing of the Declaration of Independence. It was to be a world's fair that would transform Philadelphia. Virginia's delegation, a state that boasted eight Presidents, received an invitation from the fair's organizers to submit an exhibit.

"Gari, they have invited me to be a part of the committee to decide what to send to the expo in Philadelphia," Corinne said over dinner. She showed Gari the letter from the Sesqui-Centennial committee.

"Do you think they will want me to do a painting?" Corinne asked hopefully.

"I guess you won't know until you attend this meeting," Gari said.

For Gari, these kinds of opportunities happened all the time, and they were routine for him. For Corinne they came along only rarely.

Corinne made the short trek into Fredericksburg to meet the others with whom she would be working. She carried with her a portfolio of a few of her paintings from London. At the meeting, four men and four women were seated around a table in the back of a meeting room at City Hall. She knew Mr. Humphrey and Mr. Gibbs from seeing them around town. Mr. Humphrey was tall and thin with a bald head. Mr. Gibbs was shorter with muttonchop sideburns. Corinne was the only artist.

"How about a model of Kenmore, George Washington's sister's home? That would highlight Fredericksburg," Mr. Humphrey said as soon as the meeting came to order.

"I would like to make a painting of George Washington in Philadelphia. That connects Fredericksburg to the event," Corinne offered. She began to tenderly pull out her work from London. She wished she had been the one to make the first suggestion, but men like Mr. Humphrey had no reservations about speaking up.

"If you made a model, you could make a miniature of the cherry tree and show the path that connected his boyhood farm to Kenmore," Mr. Gibbs said. Corinne gritted her teeth. Obviously, they weren't listening to her. None of the other women spoke.

Kenmore was a Georgian mansion in Fredericksburg built by George Washington's sister, Betty Washington Lewis, and her husband, Fielding Lewis. It was across a field from Ferry Farm, the estate of George Washington's mother, Mary Washington. Most schoolchildren in Virginia nicknamed the estate "Cherry Farm" according to the tradition of the cherry tree episode of Washington's youth.

"How about a painting of George Washington standing in front of a cherry tree on Ferry Farm? I could do a very large painting or even a mural. I have experience with painting murals. I brought along a few of my paintings to show you," Corinne offered again.

"We really want to highlight Kenmore. We're trying to use the Sesqui-Centennial as an opportunity to fundraise for it. A painting seems mundane," Mr. Humphrey said.

Corinne stood up from the table and stomped out of the room. She paced back and forth in the hallway to calm down. Her painting would be vibrant—definitely not mundane. The nerve! When she returned, the matter had been decided without her: they didn't want a painting.

"Mrs. Melchers, because you have an artistic background, we'd like you to be in charge of building the model," Mr. Humphrey said, oblivious to Corinne's mood. Corinne was so irritated she could barely speak. She looked around at all the smug faces in the room and slowly and deliberately packed her paintings back into her case. They hadn't even looked at them.

Back at Belmont, she fumed to Gari about the situation. "Can you imagine? They completely disregarded my idea of doing a painting, yet they want me to design the model."

"It does no good to get angry about it. The circumstances will remain the same despite this. It's not painting, but it sounds like they could use your expertise," Gari said.

For Virginia's contribution to the Sesqui-Centennial celebration, Corinne reluctantly agreed to oversee designing a one-third scale model of the back porch of Kenmore. Corinne fashioned gardens on both sides of her model and included a replica of Mary Washington's house in the distance. Her idea incorporated the porch as the point of contact between the home of Mary Washington and her daughter; in colonial times a walkway connected the two houses. Corinne wanted to highlight Fredericksburg's historic past for the visitors to Philadelphia.

Corinne titled her exhibit *Fredericksburg, George Washington's Hometown*, and after many more committee and design meetings, she delivered it to the Palace of Education in July. She and Gari rode to Philadelphia on the train to see the exhibition.

"They are making much of your display, Peachy," Gari said as he read the morning paper in their hotel. "Thousands of people have seen it."

"I'm proud of the work I did with the model, but the meetings leading up to the finished project were excruciating for me. On top of that, Kenmore had a tragic history," Corinne said.

"How so?" Gari asked.

"In my research I discovered that Fielding Lewis put so much money into the house at Kenmore that he almost went bankrupt. As a local merchant, his brother-in-law, George Washington, asked him to provide guns for the Continental Army. That took even more money away from his coffers because he was never paid for the guns. At the end of the Revolutionary War, he died a pauper, and he was buried in an unmarked grave somewhere in West Virginia," Corinne said.

"You should still be proud of your work," Gari said.

"I am happy with the attention that this model is receiving. The town may raise enough money to restore the house to its original glory—and it is connected to the Ferry Farm, which was George Washington's boyhood home," Corinne said.

"It all came together. You have really taken on Fredericksburg as your new hometown. I think Washington would be proud that the Liberty Bell is tolling again for this celebration," Gari said. "But there is some scandal that the exhibition is open on Sundays."

"Why do people have to care so much about organized religion? Go outside in the sunshine and walk in the woods or go to an exhibition celebrating this great country. Make that your church," Corinne said. Gari agreed with her despite his Catholic upbringing.

Gari and Corinne entered the expo underneath its eighty-foot replica of the Liberty Bell, covered in thousands of light bulbs. They walked along High Street, where twenty buildings had been recreated to show what they would have looked like in Colonial America; to top it all off, the street was lined with costumed tour guides. Afterwards, they headed through the exhibition to the nearby amusements at the Gladway, a carnival with concession stands on the edge of a lagoon. The Expo was designed similarly to the Pan-American Exposition they had attended ten years before in San Francisco but not quite as quaint.

Gari tried his hand at the coconut shy to win a cigar. Corinne looked on as she ate her hotdog and drank her lemonade. He paid a nickel to the carnival barker. He stood behind a fence and threw three wooden balls at coconuts on wooden stands.

"Close, but no cigar," the barker shouted.

"Let's try this next game," Corinne said.

In this one, the barker handed Gari three wooden rings. The challenge was to throw the rings so that they landed around the handles of some knives stuck in the wall. Again, he was unlucky in his endeavors.

"I will stick to painting. I'm not good at these games of chance," he said as he adjusted his straw boater hat.

"Oh, look up there!" Corinne pointed to the sky. She held onto her hat as she craned her neck, watching as an airplane sped past a silvery blimp. Abruptly, the airplane cut off its engine as it approached the blimp. It looked as if the pilot in the aircraft was talking to the pilot in the blimp's basket. The airplane re-started its engine and flew away but soon flew into a bank and looped back towards the balloon. Corinne gasped as again the pilot cut off the airplane's engine and floated so close to the blimp's basket that the pilot could have handed his handkerchief to the blimp pilot.

"What daredevils!" Gari exclaimed. Oohs and ahhs erupted from the crowd as the pilots thrilled everyone with the stunt. As much as Corinne had been irritated with the beginning of the project for the Sesqui-Centennial, now that they were at the expo, she felt like a young child drinking in all that was going on around her.

Soon Corinne's attention was drawn in another direction. She saw a small black and white collie dog and young beagle running together in a nearby field. The beagle would pop up between a couple of daisies with the collie never too far behind.

"Look, Mr. M!" Corinne said as she pointed to the dogs. "Do you think they're strays?"

Gari rolled his eyes. He knew they would take these dogs back to Belmont with them. His wife couldn't stand to see an animal in distress.

"They might get hit by a car. We should see if they are all right," Corinne said.

She ran back to the hot dog vendor and bought a couple of hot dogs. Corinne lured the dogs close enough to pet them. She plopped down on the grass beside them. In no time, the dogs were on her lap. The collie repeatedly pushed his nose up under her arm so that she would continue to stroke his fur. Corinne smiled at his antics. Soon, the beagle bayed to get some attention. Corinne laughed out loud.

"I want to take them home," Corinne said. Gari knew that Corinne never met a stray that she didn't want to save.

"How will we get them back to Belmont? We came here on the train." Gari asked.

"Send a telegram to Mr. Dillon. Ask him to come and get us in the motor car," Corinne said.

"I think you should check the local newspapers and make sure that someone isn't missing them before you abduct them to Virginia," Gari said.

"Look, they're following me. I simply must take them now," Corinne got up from her spot on the grass. Gari said nothing.

"I'll put an ad in the newspaper saying that I've found them. I'll bring them back if someone claims them, but we can't just leave them in this field to fend for themselves." The dogs happily followed her back to their hotel as she slipped them bites of hotdog all along the way.

Chapter 20

1928: Motherhood

Corinne sat on the settee in the parlor at Belmont with Polly perched on her shoulder. She wore a draped satin skirt of grey crepe with dark blue facing. Her blouse was alternating matte and shiny bands of satin. A grey felt hat dotted with French knots finished her look. Polly picked at the French knots when Corinne wasn't paying attention to her. Flash, the collie, and Spike,the beagle, lay contentedly at her feet.

Corinne listened as Gari was interviewed by yet another newspaper columnist. The interview was in response to a show that Gari was participating in in Brooklyn. Five of his paintings from the Carnegie Institute in Pittsburgh were on display at the Brooklyn Museum. Gari often asked to be excused from commenting on his artwork, but for this show, the organizers insisted he sit for an interview.

"In all the world what single thing do you find most beautiful?" The newspaper reporter asked.

"Motherhood," Gari said in a voice so low it could hardly be heard. In the silent room, Gari made a circling motion with his hand as if to describe the Earth.

"Birds and jewels and flowers delight the eye. Faces linger in the mind like music. But a mother with a baby in her arms is lovelier than all else. The tenderness of the mother, the wonder of the baby, and the intimacy of their love. That is the most beautiful thing in life," Gari said.

"In our day, very few artists have equaled your interpretation of motherhood," Corinne said.

"There is a theme of motherhood in my earliest paintings because I would paint two or three canvasses at the same time. Then I could move from one easel to another when the infant changed the pose." Gari tried to backpedal from the importance of his earlier answer.

"I suppose that motherhood is the joyous destiny of most women, and your pictures are that realization," Corinne said quietly. A tear slid down her cheek, but she quickly wiped it away so that Gari and the reporter wouldn't see it. Sometimes Gari's motherhood paintings tortured her. He had said many times that having no children was acceptable to him, but when he made these comments to reporters, she wondered if he felt differently. Regardless, the middle of an interview wasn't the place to bring it up.

"I fondly remember when the Pittsburgh Conservatory of Music held a tableau vivant, and my *Mother and Child* painting was featured. A young woman posed as the mother while another sang Woodman's "The Birthday" with piano accompaniment. Proceeds from the event were used to take tots from kindergartens in the downtown area to little excursions at beautiful gardens or nearby farms," Gari continued.

"Without the funds raised from the tableau vivant, the teachers would have been asked to pay to take the children to these places," Corinne said.

"I would have loved to paint the excursions, too," Gari said.

"Did you ever live in Pittsburgh?" The reporter asked.

"No. I made a great mistake in living most of my life abroad. Had I my life to live over again, I should go to Europe only to visit. America is where Americans belong. This is particularly true for painters. The best painter in the world can see enough beauty from his window to keep him busy a lifetime," Gari said.

"Virginia offers as many themes for art as Holland or Germany or Paris. When I am in New York, for example, riding in the subway, I see people I want to paint so much that wish becomes almost a fever. When I visited Barbados, it was my first trip to the tropics and I could barely lay down a brush," Gari continued.

"Barbados is where we got Polly," Corinne offered. Polly squawked when Corinne said her name.

"Let me tell you another topsy-turvy story about the characters in New York and why I always want to paint there. I met a patron of mine recently, a hardheaded businessman—Rotarian, Elk, that sort of thing. But he had let his hair grow so long that he looked like one of those avant-garde poets down Greenwich Village way.

'For Heaven's sake,' I said. 'Why don't you get a haircut?'

'No,' he said. 'I'm going to let it grow. Haircuts are too effeminate!'"

Gari laughed out loud. The reporter looked up from his notes at the outburst.

"On my return to Fredericksburg, I walked through the house and opened the back door. I looked down across the fields and the river. The beauty of Virginia made me wonder how I could have left it even for a winter. The natives there are quite as picturesque as I have seen in foreign lands. The women in their gingham aprons and sunbonnets. The hawk-faced men who like nothing better than to shoulder their guns, whistle for their dogs, and stray across the fields hunting," Gari continued.

"We really felt like we had come home when we moved to Belmont," Corinne added.

"I'd like to show you the studio," Gari said to the reporter. They walked across the gravel drive to the fieldstone studio. The dogs accompanied them, and Polly flew up into one of the ancient oaks on the property. The reporter tiptoed into the giant studio and approached the raised easel under the huge north window. On the easel was an oil painting of the grape arbor and house at Belmont in full spring glory with blossoming trees and bursts of yellow forsythia bushes. There were stacks of other paintings along the wall: landscapes, portraits, nudes, religious works, and studies of peasants. Gari pulled out one painting after another to show him.

"Your versatility is clear from these works," the reporter said. "Belmont is truly a shrine to art."

"Thank you," Gari said.

"And now I will take my leave. I will let you know when the story is published," the reporter said as the setting sun cast a rosy glow on the house and studio.

Now that she was approaching her fiftieth birthday, Corinne knew children were out of the question for her. Yet she still blamed herself for not giving Gari any children.

"It hurts me when you talk about motherhood with such admiration to these reporters," Corinne said when the reporter was gone.

"Oh, Peachy, that wasn't my intent. Honestly, I know it was rough for you not to have had a child. And I'm hurting with you," Gari hugged Corinne close to him.

"I find it difficult to see those paintings sometimes. Every baby in those paintings is a reminder of what we don't have," Corinne said.

"Surely you must realize there is more to you than the ability to become a mother? All the work you did for the Kenmore house at the Philadelphia Sesquicentennial? All the work you did for the Red Cross during the war? And just think about how many animals you have rescued! What would Polly, Flash, and Spike do without you?" Gari questioned.

Corinne smiled. Her husband always had a way of making her feel better. She reached down and ruffled Flash's neck as she and Gari walked arm-in-arm back into the house.

*

Within a few months, Gari traveled to New York to meet with a book publisher about a monograph of his works. When he returned to Belmont a few weeks later, he told Corinne what they had discussed. They sat together on the sofa in the living room.

"My retrospective at the Anderson Galleries deserves a proper book. Miggles is to write the text. The publisher, Rudge, suggests fifty black and white reproductions, a few color prints and some drawings or sketches interwoven. I want something more substantial than a mere collection of images. This needs to be a true art book," Gari said. The show was to fill five galleries and comprise examples of every period of his career. Corinne saw from the look in Gari's eyes how happy he was with this show and the book.

"It's wonderful that Miggles will write it. She adores you and your work, so it will be a favorable perspective. And she and Charles need the money," Corinne said. "Is there any way to include a couple facsimiles of watercolors or preliminary sketches in the book? It would give readers insight into your working process."

"I suppose that is too costly," Gari said. "Kennerly, who you know runs the Anderson Galleries, is leaving for London and will take the reproductions to Miggles,"

"I know it will tempt Miggles to include mostly works from Egmondse, as that was a special time in all our lives. She will want to write of your paintings of peasant life in Holland—the church, the fields, and the cottages. We will have to remind her to include the other periods and places," Corinne said.

"I will remind her," Gari said.

"And I do hope you'll include that sketch you did of Luek. He was such a good dog, and I still think of him." Corinne's eyes glistened with tears at the thought of her old dog.

Were the tears in her eyes for that reason alone? Corinne knew she should be happy that Miggles was writing the book for Gari, but she couldn't help feeling a little jealous of both of them. In her heart she knew that Miggles' success in writing and Gari's success in painting hadn't prevented her from being successful. Yet here she was, approaching fifty, and she hadn't submitted any paintings to the Salon or to any other large art exhibitions. She was happy for them but sad for herself.

"I will write her a letter and include this five-hundred-pound draft in exchange for the James Shannon's portrait of me. As you said, they're short on money. Kennerly would like to include it at the exhibition. If she can get more money for it by selling it to a museum, good for them. But if not, I'd like to have it so we can display it here at Belmont after the show. Do you remember James Shannon?" Gari asked.

"Of course, I remember James. Miggles and James have always been so close. He helped her out so much when George left her in Egmondse. I'm sure she would rather us have the portrait than have it in a museum," Corinne said.

"I don't remember that James helped Miggles," Gari said. His brow furrowed as he tried to remember.

"I believe he was rather sweet on Miggles," Corinne said.

"Well, it wouldn't have been the first time. He was a respondent in a divorce case in 1902, I believe. Or was it 1901?" Gari questioned himself.

"That was before my time with your friends," Corinne said. "But he was very good to Miggles when George left. He lent her money to keep her house."

"He was also a talented portrait painter. I was happy that he painted my portrait. When we couldn't afford to pay models, we used each other," Gari said.

"I love that portrait because you look so very handsome and dashing in that painting," Corinne said. Although she felt that pang of jealousy, she also felt that most of Gari's successes were hers, too. Many of her contributions led to his accomplishments.

"Thank you, my dear," Gari said.

Henrietta's book was published, and they sold copies of it at the exhibition. And the Melchers hung the James Jebusa Shannon portrait of Gari prominently in the library at Belmont.

Chapter 21

1930: The Virginia Museum of Fine Arts

Things continued to go well for Gari and Corinne as Gari gained more commissions and he could do the work at the Belmont studio rather than in New York. Henrietta's book brought him additional fans.

When their old friend, Judge John Barton Payne, finally came to visit Belmont in the spring, Gari painted his portrait. The judge was now seventy-five years old. In a blue suit and with gray hair parted down the middle, Judge Payne looked distinguished. He held his spectacles in his left hand and leaned on a green and brown winged chair with his right. Gari worked tirelessly to get all the features correct. He stayed at Belmont while Gari worked on his portrait.

Payne hoped to raise the culture of the American South. There was a complicated code of honor among white "gentlemen" and "ladies." Southern men were patriarchs in their households.

At dinner one evening after his sitting, Judge Payne spoke directly to Corinne.

"I think you're the one to help me with this problem," Judge Payne said.

"What problem?"

"I've been writing back and forth with the new Virginia governor, John Pollard, about Battle Abbey in Richmond. I do appreciate that so many school children can visit there to see my paintings. But I don't think it's a good place for my art collection. There's no fire protection, for one thing," Judge Payne said. The judge had donated fifty paintings and two busts for display in Battle Abbey.

"I had the same thought when we were there years ago for the opening," Corinne said.

"Pollard envisions a new building that would house the state's library and its new art collection comprised of my donated paintings.

The governor has poured his efforts into establishing a Virginia Museum of Fine Arts along with Alexander Weddell, who has incorporated a group of citizens into the Richmond Academy of Fine Arts. He wants to make Richmond the center of art in the South," Judge Payne said.

"Richmond is an important city, but I also think Savannah could be the center of art in the South. But where do I come into this plan?" Corinne asked.

"I'd like you to help make this all come to fruition. You did so much work for the American Red Cross and then you made that fine display for the Philadelphia celebration," Judge Payne said.

"Why haven't you asked Gari to do this?" Corinne questioned.

"I do believe that your husband is the greatest American painter since John Singer Sargent, but . . ." Judge Payne hesitated.

"You know that I've been traveling back and forth to Washington, DC to establish a National Gallery of Art. I simply don't have time to do both," Gari interrupted.

"Perhaps we can renovate the Civil War Confederate Veteran's home, next to Battle Abbey, as the permanent home of the collection. I've always felt that the veteran's home was important, but I believe there are only a few widows left there. So perhaps we could move them to another home and use the property," Corinne said.

"You see, John? That's my wife. Always thinking of solutions to problems. Never thinking that something is impossible," Gari said.

"And we want this museum to be a place where everyone is welcome. Not a place for the wealthy to show off how they are dressed," Corinne said.

In April of that year, Gari's masterpiece, *The Madonna of the Rappahannock*, was presented by Judge Payne to the State of Virginia. The painting was considered one of Gari's masterpieces, with the south side of the Rappahannock River in the background, and a Virginia matron as the model. This gift fueled Corinne's desire to see a permanent, secure home for the collection.

It was widely felt that Virginia was less hard hit by the Great Depression than other states, but the summer of 1930 brought a catastrophically severe drought to Virginia which ruined farms. Owners of apple orchards were carting barrels of water to their trees to keep them alive. Corn tassels dried up so completely that there was no pollen, which meant no corn for winter feeding. The depression had defeated many of the governor's initiatives, but he wanted the museum as a place where future generations, even in lean times, could find inspiration in great art. The museum would safeguard these treasures.

At Belmont, the heat burned the lawn to a crisp, and the flowers were ragged and drooping. The pink crepe myrtles, ordinarily lush with flowers, became sorry looking bushes. The Rappahannock River itself was very low.

Judge Payne invited Governor Pollard and the Melchers to visit his home in Washington, DC. Gari and Corinne travelled to Washington by train and stayed at a hotel. On the morning of their meeting, Gari couldn't find his shoes.

"What do you mean you can't find your shoes? We're in a hotel room. They've got to be here somewhere," Corinne said.

"I don't know where they are," Gari insisted.

"You know how I feel about being late. I don't want to be late for this meeting, even if I despise meetings," Corinne said.

"I know, you always say, 'If you're late, you're saying that you're more important than the person you're meeting,'" Gari said.

There was a knock at the hotel door and Corinne went to answer it. She returned, carrying Gari's shoes in her hands.

"Did you leave these outside the door last night to be shined for today?" she asked.

Gari looked at the shoes sheepishly. "I guess I did."

"Well, put them on so we can go. I don't want to be late," Corinne said.

When they booked the taxi at their hotel, the concierge had written "Eye" Street on a slip of paper, aware that visitors often confused DC's lettered streets. Their driver pulled up to a neoclassical home on "I" Street where children were playing on the dusty sidewalk. Corinne didn't know how the children could play in the heat. She thought they should be in the shade somewhere trying to cool off. The Melchers stepped inside Judge Payne's house to sit in the parlor and quickly delved into conversation.

"Before we begin, I'd like to offer sweet tea all around," Judge Payne said. His maid had already entered the room holding a tray with a pitcher and some glasses. She passed around a glass of tea to each of them.

"If we are to provide adequate housing for Virginia's works of art, we must build a separate building for that purpose. I will consent to giving $100,000," Judge Payne said.

"But we'll need twice that amount for an adequate museum," Governor Pollard said. He drummed his fingers on the arm of the sofa. The governor had a jutting chin and thin straight mouth. It seemed to Corinne that they had already been discussing this before she and Gari entered the house.

"Perhaps there's someone else who would also donate $100,000," Judge Payne said.

"You all know the philanthropists of Virginia. Who might be interested in art?" Pollard asked.

"It is very difficult to know who has money, as persons who were well to do in 1929 are now having difficulty meeting their obligations," Judge Payne said.

"Had this opportunity arisen before 1929 we probably could have found someone who would have been glad to make a substantial donation, but with the dark outlook before us, I don't think anyone will make a huge commitment," Gari said.

"Let's adopt a new strategy then. Let's solicit smaller pledges of, say, $5000 to $25,000," Governor Pollard said.

"For a larger pledge, we could give a donor the opportunity to name a memorial gallery," Corinne offered.

"That's a brilliant idea," Governor Pollard said. He talked as though a weight had been lifted from his shoulders. "I will organize a founders committee and Corinne, you will be a part of it."

"I want this museum to become the South's greatest art institution," Corinne said. They raised their glasses to that.

*

When the couple returned to Belmont, Corinne set to work. The proposed site for the museum was the R. E. Lee Camp Confederate Soldiers' Home, a large residential complex for poor and infirm Southern veterans of the Civil War. The twenty-four-acre property was bounded by the Boulevard, Grove Avenue, Shepherd Street, and Kensington Avenue in Richmond. The superintendent's home, nine residential cottages, and a chapel were in this oak-filled park. The State of Virginia had always funded this property, and it was agreed that the property would return to the state when the present purpose of housing the veterans was no longer needed. These buildings were to be destroyed by the founder's committee for the museum.

Corinne would only agree on the plan if they also built a Home for Confederate Women, a residence for destitute female relatives of Confederate soldiers. She knew there were several women still in need of housing. She traveled to Richmond and met with a few of the surviving widows. There had been numerous cases of elderly Civil War veterans marrying young girls to act as their caregivers by promising the young brides their pensions. The pensions were one of the few steady forms of income during the Depression.

"Mrs. Melchers, I'd like to introduce you to Alberta Stewart from Alabama," the director said. Mrs. Stewart was elderly and terribly thin, likely weighing less than one-hundred pounds. She perched in a wheelchair with her tiny feet barely touching the floor. A small Confederate battle flag fluttered from the back handle of her chair.

"I get fifty dollars a month from my husband's pension, but that's not near enough to live on," Mrs. Stewart said, once the two women had been introduced.

"Did your husband talk much about the war?" Corinne knelt beside the wheelchair.

"No, he didn't talk much about it. Except for the battle of Petersburg that lasted for ten months. They were in trenches full of water, and it was rough. Hungry all the time. They came across a potato patch one time and made up some mashed potatoes to eat. That was all they had for days," Mrs. Stewart said.

"Did you love your husband?" Corinne asked. Corinne knew that there was a huge age difference in the pair. Her husband had been in his late eighties when he made arrangements with the family to marry the fifteen-year-old Alberta.

"That's a hard question to answer. He had a bad temper. I was much younger than him and he didn't want nobody messing with me. He had striking blue eyes," Mrs. Stewart said.

Corinne patted Mrs. Stewart's hand and rose to talk to the director again.

"It will be a joy to help our Mrs. Stewart and all the other women," Corinne said.

Corinne worked with the architect to design a neoclassical home for the widows that resembled the White House, and it was to be built on the west side of the property simultaneous to the museum build. Corinne also wanted to preserve the Confederate Memorial Chapel. A beautiful white building served as a place of worship for the residents of the home. The pews were hand-hewn, and the building had eight stained glass windows dedicated to the soldiers and battalions of the Confederacy. Many Confederate funerals had been held there. The Stars and Bars flag of the Confederacy flew above the chapel.

Corinne had spread the pages of her notes for the project all around her writing room.

"Just dust around the pages, Sarah," Corinne said as Sarah entered the room with her bucket of supplies to clean.

"Yes, Mrs. Melchers," Sarah said.

Corinne enjoyed the work on the museum project, but she found herself squeezing her painting into the small bits of time that were left at the end of the day. Her patience, energy, and creative flow were tapped out by the many meetings she had to attend for the museum, and the pieces she painted felt flat and uninspired. Painting had always made her feel grounded and happy. As challenging and rewarding as the museum project was, she needed to get back into her own creative flow.

Chapter 22

1932: The Death

Despite the country being in the midst of the Great Depression, the 1932 Summer Olympics went on as planned in Los Angeles. As had been the case since the 1912 Olympics, there were art competitions in architecture, music, literature, painting, and sculpture for works inspired by sports.

While sitting on a rocking chair on Belmont's front porch one summer day, Gari and Corinne discussed whether Gari should enter his painting of the life-sized fencer.

"Peachy, it's not a new painting. It's from 1895," Gari said.

"I realize it's not new. But it certainly shows a fencer in great form," Corinne replied.

"My friend, Ernest Noir, was the model. He was a painter, too. We modeled for each other back in the day. I don't think you ever met him," Gari reminisced.

"No, I never met him. You could enter the painting hors concours and not compete for a prize. But people could see it, and that's the important thing," Corinne said.

"I suppose that's true. Even if it was eligible for a medal, in the arts competitions the judges don't always award the prizes. If they feel the work is not worthy of gold, silver, or bronze, they award nothing," Gari said.

"If I had a painting of something sports related, I would enter it. But sports just aren't my forte," Corinne said. Gari laughed aloud at the pun.

"I thought that would get a chuckle from you. From what I understand, the music competitions are even more harshly judged than the arts and literature. The musical works aren't performed at the Olympics, they're submitted on paper. Imagine how difficult that is to judge, just looking at the notes and trying to hear it in your head," Corinne said.

"Perhaps I'll send the painting out to Los Angeles. But I don't feel up to traveling out there myself. The phlebitis in my legs makes it so difficult for me," Gari said, grasping his cane with a liver-spotted hand to emphasize his point.

Corinne had noticed that her husband relied on his cane more and more frequently to walk from place to place. His hair had thinned considerably. He enjoyed sitting out on the porch in the rocking chairs more than sitting on the chair next to his easel.

The Los Angeles Museum hosted the Olympic art exhibition, which was not a part of the Olympic sports venues. Hostesses attired in native costumes sashayed through each of the rooms where sculptures and paintings of various national groups were exhibited. Enormous crowds jammed the museum galleries to take in the color and charm. Corinne read in the newspaper that Lee Blair of Los Angeles won first place for his watercolor *Rodeo*. The former Ruth Miller, Mrs. Henry Fracker, of East Orange, NJ, won second place for her massive painting of two wrestlers, one black and one white, *Struggle*. Corinne wondered how Ruth felt about becoming Mrs. Henry Fracker—if losing her identity to marriage bothered her as much as it had bothered Corinne. There was no bronze medal winner. The twenty-year-old Lee Blair became very emotional when he stood on the podium. The announcer intoned his name, and the "Star-Spangled Banner" played as the American flag was hoisted up the flagpole. Corinne could picture it.

In early November, when the Olympics were long over, a retrospective of Gari's art opened at the American Academy of Arts and Letters in the Washington Heights area of New York City. The exhibition opened on November 1, 1932 and included paintings from his first successes up to the present. The exhibition showed that Gari held his own within his body of work despite the changing ideals and fashion of the art world. Fauvism and Cubism peaked in 1914 at the start of the Great War; the Dada movement was a reaction to the horrors of war. After the war, the Bauhaus and Expressionism surged in Germany while American Modernism displayed optimism for the future in the United States.

While he was in New York, Corinne was at Belmont preparing the house for Thanksgiving. She supervised the cleaning of the house, the killing of one of her beloved turkeys, and the baking of mince and pumpkin pies.

Gari returned from New York in time to sit in the dining room in front of their huge *Market Scene* still life painting and eat Thanksgiving dinner with Corinne. The couple enjoyed looking at the row of their collection of delft teapots displayed across the fireplace mantle. From the flea markets in Egmondse, Gari recalled buying each one. He had traveled back and forth to New York so much that he treasured these moments at home.

"I made an appointment for us to have some Christmas portraits taken at the beginning of December," Corinne said.

"I know how much you love Christmas. I look forward to sitting beside you, my dear," Gari cut a piece of turkey from his plate. The green asparagus tips, red cranberry sauce, and golden orange sweet potatoes on his plate were nearly as colorful as their large dining room still life. Although he ate heartily, he looked more tired than normal. His skin was so pale.

"Wait. We have so much to be thankful for, and we forgot to say that at the beginning of the meal," Corinne said.

"I couldn't help digging in," Gari said as he put down his fork and picked up his wine glass with one hand. With the other, he reached for Corinne's hand and intertwined his fingers with hers. She noticed the paint stains, so similar to his hands during their first dinner together on the ship so many years before. But she also noticed his paper-thin skin and the spiderweb of veins across his hands.

"Thanksgiving is a time to reflect on our blessings. We're blessed to live in this beautiful home, and we have each other and our pets," Gari said. Corinne nodded her head.

Just then a sunbeam entered the dining-room window. Bright circles of light landed on their dining room table and turned their plates of food into glistening jewels.

"Sunlight," Corinne said. "I'm thankful for sunlight." She knew both she and Gari were thinking about painting the scene before them.

A few days later in the early morning, Corinne heard Gari's breathing change, and she knew something was wrong. She ran to his room.

The dogs' nails scratched the floorboards as they tried to get out of her way. She cradled his head in her arms and kissed his pale face.

"Breathe. Please breathe," she said to him. She thought he would wake up and everything would be fine. She ran to push the button on the wall to call her housekeeper.

"Sarah!" she yelled when Sarah didn't respond to the call button. She then turned her attention back to Gari.

"I'm here. I love you. I always will," she whispered into his ear. She felt his heart stop beating and his body begin to turn waxy and cold.

She sat on the bed next to him, stroking the familiar wrinkles on his face. Sarah came into the room and held Corinne's other hand. The maid was amazingly calm as she looked at her boss's lifeless body. Corinne stretched out on the bed next to her husband. She looked out the window to see a red-tailed hawk soaring above the Rappahannock River on its way southward.

Gari died from a massive heart attack on November 30th, 1932. Corinne eventually talked to his doctor at the hospital.

"He was sick with phlebitis, and I diagnosed him with blood clots in his veins. Probably one of the blood clots traveled to his heart," the doctor explained. Corinne sent a telegram to London.

> MIGGLES
>
> REGRET TO INFORM YOU THAT GARI HAS PASSED AWAY ON NOVEMBER 30. STOP. I HOPE I HAVE THE STRENGTH TO BEAR THIS. STOP. PLEASE COME AS SOON AS POSSIBLE. STOP. FUNERAL WILL BE DECEMBER 2. STOP.
>
> CORINNE

*

Corinne Melcher held her husband's funeral services at Belmont on December 2nd at 11:00 a.m. Reverend Dudley, rector of St. George's Episcopal Church, conducted the service, and a baritone sang two of Gari's favorite hymns. It was a small, private service, as Gari had requested. Corinne's brothers, Leonard and Lawton, were there along with the servants. Gari Melcher's body was taken to Washington DC afterwards to be cremated, as was his wish.

"Not a moment goes by that I don't think about him," Corinne said to Leonard after the funeral. Tears spilled from her eyes as she spoke. She found comfort in having her older brother by her side. "What am I going to do?"

"You and Gari built this beautiful farm and studio together, and you enjoyed it together. I'm sorry for your sadness, but the studio will always be a happy place, full of precious memories. You'll continue to work here," Leonard said to his sister. Shortly after the funeral her brothers left, and Miggles hadn't yet arrived. Corinne was exhausted.

"Please don't tell me he's in a better place. I don't want him in a better place. I want him here. With me. Right now," Corinne said over and over to Sarah. Sarah listened patiently to her mistress. Corinne felt guilty for being the one still alive, and she also was angry at Gari for leaving her. *I have to believe that there are brighter days ahead. Everything will sort itself out. This will all bring me closer to where I want to go. I just have to learn to live with missing him.* Thoughts like these circled constantly through Corinne's grieving mind.

The world continued, except Corinne no longer had Gari beside her. His art show in New York City remained open, but the members hung a black crepe banner over the door. Groups of high school students continued to visit the exhibit to study his paintings.

When Corinne ventured into town to shop for groceries, something she had done alone many times when Gari was off traveling, she now felt as though everyone watched her. People seemed awkward and didn't know what to say to her. At home, Corinne would curl up in Gari's bathrobe because it still smelled faintly of his aftershave. There were moments when Corinne would think, *I can't wait to tell Gari about this.* She would then remember that he was gone. He wasn't just away attending to an installation; he wouldn't walk through the door again.

The moment Henrietta and Charles crossed Belmont's threshold, Corinne fell into Henrietta's arms and sobbed. Henrietta was quiet and held her friend. Corinne felt like a fragile bird in her arms; she had lost so much weight.

"I'm so sorry. What can I do for you?" Henrietta asked.

"Just you being here helps," Corinne said through tears.

"I'm here to listen. And to do whatever you need me to do," Henrietta said. "The first thing we're going to do is get you something to eat."

"I'm not hungry." Corinne dragged her feet as she followed Henrietta and Charles into the dining room.

"Well, you'll sit with us while we eat. Maybe Sarah can whip something up that will entice you to eat with us," Henrietta said.

*

To assuage her grief, Corinne plunged into work at Belmont. She added a hexagonal sun porch to the Belmont house. She also added a summer house, a barn, and a stone garage.

She completed her work on the Virginia Museum of Fine Arts in Richmond. In Gari's honor, she solicited multiple members of the art community to pledge and name memorial galleries, and they fulfilled their promises. She desperately wanted to preserve her husband's legacy.

Corinne began planning for the future, and she needed Henrietta as a sounding board. One morning, as they sat in the new sunroom drinking their coffee, Corinne voiced her plans.

"Gari's hardly known here in the United States, even though he's had so many honors abroad," Corinne said. Henrietta looked up from her coffee.

"It feels as though as a nation, the United States is almost indifferent to the achievements of its citizens in the arts and letters."

"We've discussed this before. You know that, Corinne," Henrietta said, wondering where Corinne was taking this conversation.

"He has paintings in the Metropolitan Museum of Art. He has murals in the Congressional Library. His portrait of President Roosevelt hangs in the Smithsonian Institution. He is an officer of the French Legion of Honor, and has been decorated by Prussia, Bavaria, and Saxe-Weimar," Corinne added. "I'm going to turn the studio and grounds into a museum of his art."

"I think that's a marvelous idea," Henrietta said. "Converting Belmont into a museum would do more than preserve his art. It would give people a sense of his daily life as an artist. That's something you can't get from just seeing his work in a gallery."

Corinne began buying back any of his paintings that were available, and she kept the ones that were already at Belmont. She envisioned people walking through the studio and picturing Gari sitting in the chair next to the easel, just as she herself did nearly every day.

Chapter 23
1935: Validation

Gari was gone, and it was time for Corinne to pursue her dream of becoming an artist in her own right. She was an incredible painter. She needed to believe in her dream even if it felt hard. She felt loneliness but she simultaneously wanted to represent her own agency.

On February 4th, she attended the Bal Boheme in Washington DC as the guest of C. Powell Minnigerode, the director of the Corcoran Gallery of Art. The gallery was considered to be the most important art museum in Washington, especially for American art. Gari had exhibited at the Corcoran many times throughout his career.

The costume ball's theme was "In the Orient;" it didn't begin until almost midnight. The musicians wore huge turbans decorated with jewels. They played a processional titled "Marco Polo Revisits the Orient," as the guests marched around the ballroom. Huge masks and Chinese lanterns hung above the tables. The walls were painted with Tibetan gates, and colorful streamers flowed from the chandeliers. A large papier mâché Buddha occupied the south end of the ballroom.

Corinne's costume was a genie from a bottle. Her dress had layers and layers of light blue silk. She wore golden slippers. She completed the look with a veil across her face.

"Mrs. Melchers, it's so good to see that you accepted my invitation and are out enjoying yourself. We were all so sorry to hear about Gari's passing," Powell Minnigerode said.

"Thank you, Mr. Minnigerode. My husband always spoke highly of you," Corinne said.

"Please, call me Powell."

"Very well then, Powell. And you may call me Corinne," Corinne said.

Later in the evening, Corinne ran into Powell once again. He leaned next to a doorway, watching as the guests danced.

"Corinne, the art world misses your prolific husband's paintings," Powell said. He sipped from his champagne flute.

"They don't have to miss out on Melchers' paintings altogether," Corinne said.

"How so?"

"I paint as well. Throughout my life I have struggled to be taken seriously as an artist. I had to give up so much for him. I've always been in Gari's shadow," Corinne said. Corinne didn't feel self-conscious about promoting her own artwork, perhaps due to the champagne,

"I would love to see some of your paintings. Would it be possible for you to bring a portfolio to my office in DC? The biennial is next month and perhaps we could include some. The American public would appreciate another Melchers," Powell said.

Corinne traveled to Washington DC with her paintings just as she had done so long ago when she took her paintings to Paris. She met Minnegerode in the gallery.

"These paintings are evidence of your talent. The soft, varied brushstrokes present a dreamlike quality to this one," Powell said about *The Pink Room.*

"I love them all. My art is me. What is happening on the surface of the canvas is a reflection of me."

True to his word, in March 1935, Corinne was invited by Mr. C. Powell Minnigerode to exhibit several of her paintings in the Corcoran Biennial Exhibition of American Painting. She chose *The Pink Room* that she had painted in 1910 as one of the paintings to exhibit. She also included two of the paintings she had done in London.

She had painted an Impressionist landscape of Belmont with her beloved Ivy in the foreground. She remembered how she had struggled to paint the fur correctly. She also included the still life of flowers with the coral necklace. In spirit, the still life felt much like the painting she had done the first time she had submitted her work for the Paris Salon. She hoped the public would enjoy them as much as she had enjoyed painting them.

When Corinne returned to Belmont after the opening, she read a *Richmond Times-Dispatch* review of the show.

"Corinne Melchers (Mrs. Gari Melchers), a member of the Virginia Arts Commission," the art critic wrote, "is represented by a charming interior *The Pink Room* in soft tones of rose and ivory." He did not mention the other two paintings. She folded the paper and threw it down on the breakfast table.

"Why do they have to identify me in parentheses as Mrs. Gari Melchers? Why can't I be Corinne Melchers, a member of the Virginia Arts Commission? I was a painter before I was Mrs. Gari Melchers. I was a painter while I was Mrs. Gari Melchers. I will always be a painter. I thought if I worked harder or tried harder, it would make a difference. Even in death he outshines me," she said out loud to her parrot. Polly squawked.

Sarah could hear Corinne ranting from the kitchen.

"No mention of the other two paintings, either. I felt they were just as strong as *The Pink Room*," she mumbled to herself.

When the show was over, she rode the train to Washington to retrieve the paintings. When she returned to Belmont, she had Mr. Dillon light a large bonfire in the yard by the smokehouse. The border collie and beagle that she had rescued in Pennsylvania were still by her side. They played in the yard around the fire.

"Leave me some wood, and I'll keep the fire going myself, Mr. Dillon," Corinne pulled her shawl closer around her shoulders in the cool evening.

"If you're sure you'll be alright, Ma'am," he said.

"I'll be fine. I haven't seen my dogs in a few days, and I'd like to spend some time outside with them," Corinne reached down to scratch the beagle's neck.

After Corinne saw the lights switch off in Mr. Dillon's house and she was sure he was asleep, she went inside the studio and gathered all the paintings she had done while in London. One by one, she threw them into the fire. The smoke and embers swirled around her head. The flames grew higher and brighter with each canvas she tossed in. These paintings were a testament to a world that didn't understand her. She cried as the flames engulfed each painting. The soot from the fire smeared with her tears.

From her room, Sarah saw the bright glow from the fire. Once in the kitchen, she looked out the window and saw her mistress. Sarah threw on her robe hastily, snuck into the studio, and grabbed six of the closest paintings she could find. With the canvases gathered in the skirts of her robe, she made her way back to the kitchen, remaining in the shadows so that Corinne couldn't see her. She stashed the paintings away in the pantry.

The next morning, Corinne slowly came to the in the dining room table for breakfast. Her hair was disheveled, and her eyes were puffy and red. What had she done? She dropped into one of the dining room chairs and held her head in one hand. Sarah tiptoed into the dining room and poured her mistress a cup of coffee. The house was eerily quiet.

"Ma'am, I know you don't want to hear this now. But you have had a remarkable life. You know it in your heart," Sarah whispered. "You live in this beautiful house. You have wonderful friends. And your paintings are beautiful. You don't need anyone else to tell you that." The sound of her voice startled Corinne.

"I want to believe you," Corinne said. "But I burned all my paintings last night. I thought I could hide my broken heart in the flames. I was silly to think I could compare to my husband. Supporting his career was demanded of me as a wife, and I resented him for it. But I'm going to spend the rest of my days making sure that Gari's memory lives on."

"Making sure that Mr. M lives on in his paintings is fine. But I saved a couple 'a your paintings. And I'm going to have Mr. Dillon hang'em up in this house—especially that *Pink Room* one," Sarah said.

"Sarah, you've been with me for twenty years, and you're too kind to me. The person I was meant to be is gone. I gave her up long ago," Corinne said. She took Sarah's two hands in her own and pressed them against her forehead. Sarah gently slipped from Corinne's grasp and went back into the kitchen. When she returned, she had something hidden behind her back.

"I think you're going to be especially happy that I saved this one," Sarah said, revealing the portrait that Corinne had painted of her husband. The painting featured an older, greying Gari; he stood next to his easel, painting one of his Dutch models. Her husband always had a paintbrush in his hand. He was so involved in his own painting that he hadn't even noticed that Corinne creating the portrait. The painting also showed the Dutch model in a mirror on the wall. It was quite an accomplished painting.

"I do love that painting. That's how I want to remember him. Did you know I met Mr. M on the ship taking my paintings to the Paris Salon? He helped me take them to the Louvre. Painting was always my first real love. I always thought I would reunite with it, and this show at the Corcoran was going to be my chance. Maybe the best part of me is dead, and I must come to terms with that." Corinne paused. "But thank you for saving them . . . especially this one, Sarah." Corinne sat a little taller in her seat and sipped her cup of coffee. Sarah propped the painting on the dining room chair across from Corinne. It was as if Gari was once again joining her for breakfast on a quiet morning.

"I admire your loyalty to Mr. M., you've become stronger since his death. You have the determination to do whatever you want. I see it in you," Sarah said.

Corinne nodded in agreement. Sarah began flipping through a small pile of mail.

"And this came in the mail for you while you were away," Sarah said. The return address on the letter was from the Virginia Museum of Fine Arts.

> Dear Mrs. Gari Melchers,
>
> So strong is our feeling that we are impelled to phrase our gratitude to you for exhibiting your paintings at the Corcoran Biennial. If you haven't committed the painting to anyone else, we would like to purchase the painting titled *Interior* for our permanent collection.
>
> Committee for Acquisitions

"Sarah, you have to sit and join me," Corinne said. She could hardly believe what she was reading. "The museum that I helped design and bring to life wants to display one of my paintings."

Sarah sat at the table beside Corinne. She poured herself a cup of coffee.

"Cheers," Sarah said, lifting her cup.

"Cheers." Corinne clinked her coffee cup to Sarah's.

It was unnecessary to compare herself to her husband. His artistic strengths and talents didn't take away from hers. She wished that her sacrifices had been more appreciated in his lifetime, but perhaps now that was happening. *Why couldn't a wife be a husband's best friend and confidante? Why couldn't the two, by combining their energies, make their lives count for more than either one could by themselves?* Corinne thought. She still desired for the world to recognize her as more than an artist's wife.

"I only ever wanted to paint," Corinne said softly, looking at the painting of Gari across from her. "Nothing more than that."

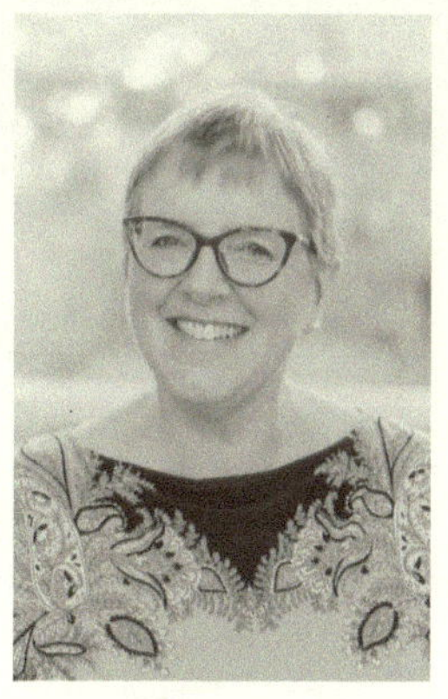

About the Author

Joyce A. Miller is an author based in the Church Hill section of Richmond, Virginia. She has written and indie-published two books: *Joe Harris, the Moon* is historical fiction based on the true story of Miller's granduncle who played baseball in the 1910s/1920s, and *Look! You're Dancing: A Memoir of Dogs, Dance and Devotion*, a memoir of Miller's adoption journey of six greyhounds. Miller is an active member of James River Writers and the Church Hill Book Club. Before she started writing, Miller worked for over thirty years as a mechanical designer at a nuclear physics laboratory.

www.ingramcontent.com/pod-product-compliance
Lightning Source LLC
LaVergne TN
LVHW051000080826
845145LV00009B/2383

* 9 7 8 1 9 6 6 3 6 9 4 0 0 *